"Come on, Laura, cut me some slack—unless you're afraid of me."

"You just startled me, that's all." Laura smiled, unable to stop comparing Nick to one of her students. They got lost sometimes, basically good kids who lost all sense of themselves and what was important. And those who didn't care about themselves were the ones who made disastrous mistakes with their lives.

So exactly how did one go about cutting some slack to a dangerously handsome man who reminded her alternately of the devil himself and a lost little boy? Laura collected kids in need the way some people picked up stray cats and took them home with them; she certainly couldn't start treating grown men the same way. Although, for a second, the thought of taking Nick home with her had her heart kicking into high gear....

Dear Reader,

The weather may be cooling off as fall approaches, but the reading's as hot as ever here at Silhouette Intimate Moments. And for our lead title this month I'm proud to present the first longer book from reader favorite BJ James. In *Broken Spurs* she's created a hero and heroine sure to live in your mind long after you've turned the last page.

Karen Leabo returns with *Midnight Confessions*, about a bounty hunter whose reward—love—turns out to be far different from what he'd expected. In *Bringing Benjy Home*, Kylie Brant matches a skeptical man with an intuitive woman, then sets them on the trail of a missing child. *Code Name: Daddy* is the newest Intimate Moments novel from Marilyn Tracy, who took a break to write for our Shadows line. It's a unique spin on the ever-popular "secret baby" plotline. And you won't want to miss *Michael's House*, Pat Warren's newest book for the line and part of her REUNION miniseries, which continues in Special Edition. Finally, in *Temporary Family* Sally Tyler Hayes creates the family of the title, then has you wishing as hard as they do to make the arrangement permanent.

Enjoy them all—and don't forget to come back next month for more of the best romance fiction around, right here in Silhouette Intimate Moments.

Leslie Wainger

Leslie Wainger,
Senior Editor and Editorial Coordinator

Please address questions and book requests to:
Silhouette Reader Service
U.S.: 3010 Walden Ave., P.O. Box 1325, Buffalo, NY 14269
Canadian: P.O. Box 609, Fort Erie, Ont. L2A 5X3

TEMPORARY FAMILY

SALLY TYLER HAYES

Published by Silhouette Books

America's Publisher of Contemporary Romance

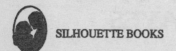 SILHOUETTE BOOKS

ISBN 0-373-07738-6

TEMPORARY FAMILY

SALLY TYLER HAYES

lives in South Carolina with her husband, son and daughter. A former journalist for a South Carolina newspaper, she fondly remembers that her decision to write and explore the frontiers of romance came at about the same time she discovered, in junior high, that she'd never be able to join the crew of the Starship Enterprise.

Happy and proud to be a stay-home mom, she is thrilled to be living her lifelong dream of writing romance fiction.

Sally loves to hear from readers. You may write to her at P.O. Box 5452 (A), Greenville, SC 29606.

This book is for a special friend, Cynthia.
It's so nice to have a friend whose love for books
matches my own. It makes me so happy to talk books
with you, hunt for books with you and go away to
conferences with you. And when I die, my copy of
Mackenzie's Mountain is yours.

Chapter 1

The ringing of the phone woke Dr. Nicholas Garrett from a sound sleep. Groggily, he rubbed his sore neck. He'd fallen asleep on the couch again, where a man of his size had no hope of sleeping comfortably. Still, it was sleep—something he didn't take for granted anymore.

He glanced at his watch. It was almost two o'clock. But two in the morning or the afternoon? He looked out the window. Afternoon, he decided, not caring that the sky was overcast or that no hint of sunshine poked through the clouds. He wasn't going anywhere.

Nick grabbed the phone, which wouldn't stop ringing. "Yes."

"Lord, Nick, you sound like a grumpy old bear," a husky voice teased.

He recognized the voice immediately. It was A.J., the woman he'd been in love with for the better part of the past six years. She was married to another man now, and she was carrying that man's child. Nick wished that was his only problem right now, but it was just the beginning.

"Nick? Are you still there? It's almost party time," she said. "You didn't forget, did you?"

He hadn't forgotten the kids at the shelter were giving A.J. a baby shower, but he hadn't planned to go. He hadn't walked inside the doors of Hope House in . . . he had to stop to think.

What month was this?

He looked at the date window on his watch. *May?*

That seemed impossible—it had been nearly a year. He'd somehow lost track of the passage of time since then, though he could have rattled off the date, the hour, the minute when everything in life had started to go so wrong for him. And for one innocent child.

"You promised you'd be here, Nick," A.J. reminded him.

"I know," he said impatiently. How long had it been since he'd even gone out of the apartment? He couldn't remember. He managed to hide himself away for days at a time now. No one bothered him anymore, except A.J.

"I've kept my part of the bargain. I haven't called and bugged you about anything in two weeks."

"And I'm grateful for that," he said sincerely. He wanted to tell her he wouldn't be there, but he wasn't sure he could afford to do that. He'd isolated himself in this apartment, cut himself off from everything and everyone associated with his work. And he was starting to scare even himself.

He was depressed. He certainly didn't need a psychiatrist to tell him. After all, he was a psychiatrist.

And the woman on the other end of the phone wanted him to walk back into Hope House? He shook his head. A sarcastic smile spread across his lips. She might as well ask him to fly to the moon.

"Nick?" she prompted, impatient as always.

"I'm working on it, A.J.," he said, being more honest with her than he had been in months. It *was* work. Just to think about walking inside that place again and seeing those kids who needed so many things from him, which he didn't have to give anymore, was hard as hell.

"Please, Nick. Something has come up, and...I need your help, all right?"

"You can talk to me on the phone," he said. "I don't have to come down there."

"It wouldn't be the same. Besides, if you don't make it down here today, I might resort to blowing up your apartment just to get you out of there," she warned, then hung up the phone before he could object again.

He pictured the place exploding around him and wondered where he would hide then.

Two hours later, Nick stood outside the shelter for runaways for what seemed like forever, watching the kids stream inside.

He felt as helpless as any of them. Over the past year, he'd lost faith in his ability to help those kids, lost his belief that he could honestly make a difference in any of their lives. And he didn't know how to get that back—or if it was even possible.

He didn't know if he wanted to practice psychiatry again, because right now the risks felt too great. He'd screwed up, and the kids had paid for it. He couldn't take chances like that again. So he stayed across the street, under the awning of some abandoned storefront, and managed to stay fairly dry. The cold and the wind didn't bother him at all.

Hope House was lit up like a Christmas tree tonight. Though his watch assured him it was May now, someone had pulled a few strands of Christmas lights out of storage and strung them around the entrance. It was for the party, no doubt, but the effect was strange. He'd spotted the lights two blocks away. Hundreds of small white bulbs, flickering off and on, guiding him through the night, calling him home, it seemed. Why did coming here feel like coming home to him, when all he wanted to do was forget?

Nick had never lived here, but he'd offered the kids his help for free—when he could find one who was willing to talk to him and listen to what he had to say. Tonight, watching the kids streaming inside, recognizing one here and there, he realized how much he'd missed the place, even if he was petrified of going inside.

When he finally found the courage to walk through the front door, Carlos, a skinny little kid with a blackened eye and a cast on his arm, noticed him right away.

"Dr. Nick, my man." Carlos slapped him on the back.

Nick tried not to think how long it had been since anyone had called him "Dr. Nick." "Hey, what happened to the arm and the eye?"

"You know how it is, Dr. Nick."

He nodded. He certainly did. Carlos had a mean-tempered uncle who took his frustrations out on him on those rare occasions when Carlos happened to be at home.

"You stayin' for the party?"

"Maybe." Nick wasn't quite ready to commit to that. "I have to talk to A.J. first about something, but . . . maybe I'll see you later, before I leave."

As Nick hurried down the hall, his heart rate was higher than it should be, his throat a little tight. But he'd done it; he'd walked through the door. He rounded the corner and bumped right into A.J. going ninety miles an hour without looking where she was heading.

"Easy," he said, grabbing her arms to keep her upright.

She gasped in surprise, then smiled. "Nick, I can't believe you made it."

"When you were so sweet to invite me?" He feigned shock. Humor was all he had left, that and a bit of cynicism. Besides, that was how it had always been between A.J. and him. He hoped they could at least hang on to their old, easy friendship now that she'd married Jack MacAlister.

"I missed you, Nick. Now, come upstairs," she said. "I have a little problem, and I need your help."

"I came here for a party," he said, following her.

"Did you really believe that?" she shot back. "Nick, I'm surprised at you. I didn't invite you here to have fun. I invited you to work."

Nick wasn't laughing. He hadn't worked in a year, and A.J. knew that. He wasn't going back to work. Not yet. Maybe not ever.

A.J. climbed the stairs. Hope House had a handful of staff members who lived on the site. A.J. used to be one of them. She led him into what used to be her old room. Before he could stop her, she turned on the light, roused a child and started to introduce them.

"Wait a minute," he said from the doorway, louder and more harshly than he should have, reacting out of sheer fear alone.

The little boy on the bed made a choked-off squawking sound—clearly one of fright—and Nick cursed himself in a low, bitter voice.

It all happened so fast he hadn't even had time to think about what he was doing. And he didn't think he'd ever been so scared in his life—all because he was being asked to go back to work before he was ready.

Now he'd scared the boy. A.J. shot Nick a venomous look, then went to soothe the child for a moment before coming back to the doorway.

"I'm sorry," he said, before she could tell him what a jerk he was.

She stared at him for a long time, and he wondered what she saw.

"You look like hell, Nick."

He supposed that pretty much summed it up—whether she was talking about his physical appearance or what she could see in his eyes. He'd been to hell and he couldn't hide that, especially not from A.J.

"I apologize," he said, sorry for what he'd done. He didn't give a damn how he looked.

"I've got trouble in there," she said, nodding toward the room.

"Get someone else, A.J." He would have begged her if he thought it would do any good.

"I can't find anyone else. Dr. Jamison was called to Cook County Hospital on an emergency. Dr. Carter is on vacation, and I haven't found another backup for us yet. Besides, no one else can do this job the way you did.''

''Tell me another one,'' he said.

She dared to smile. ''No one else works as cheaply as you do.''

He couldn't argue with that; he'd worked for nothing. But he couldn't do the work anymore. Nick felt the sickness that always came with that admission wash over him yet again.

''Please,'' she said. ''He's so little, and he's scared. He hasn't said a word to us since he's been here. He's obviously been out on the streets for a couple of days, but I don't think he's a runaway. I think he's in shock, Nick.''

''He's too young to be here—you know that. You can't call a child his age a runaway. Phone Child and Family Services, and let them handle it.''

''I will. I'll do it right now, but how long do you think it will take social services to get him to a psychiatrist?''

She had a point there. The county never had the money or the manpower to do the job that needed to be done for these kids. That was where Hope House came in.

''Just talk to him,'' she said. ''Or see if you can get him to talk. We found him sitting in a corner on the floor downstairs. He was dripping wet, shivering, starving.''

''And he hasn't said a thing?''

''Not a single word. Nick?''

''Yes?''

''There was blood on his shoes and on the cuffs of his jeans.''

A.J. had asked Nick to do something quite simple. He didn't have to solve all of this kid's problems. She just wanted him to get the kid to talk, to find out what happened to him and get the name of someone she could call to come pick up the boy, rather than turn him over to the social-services system.

He watched while A.J. explained what was going on to the boy, introduced Nick as a friend of hers, then promised Nick would bring the boy to the party when they were done. Cake, ice cream, cookies—surely they would be incentive enough to make him talk. A.J. fled the scene before Nick could protest further.

Nick turned and looked at the boy, who gave him one of the saddest looks he had ever seen. The boy's eyes seemed to have sunk into his face, a sign of extreme fatigue, but the lashes were thick and curly. His skin was a warm, muted brown, his hair a mass of short-clipped curls lying nearly flat against his head. His arms were thin and long, his fingers clenched on top of the blanket.

Don't think about it, Nick reminded himself. Don't try to figure out where he's been, how he's been hurt, why no one is around to take care of him or what might happen once he leaves the shelter. Those were the kinds of questions he had no business asking himself. Not anymore.

So Nick stood there in the doorway, telling himself this was just another lost kid. The shelter was full of them. This boy wasn't his responsibility. Most likely, the kid was already broken deep inside in some vital way, and it wasn't Nick's fault if he couldn't perform miracles and put this little boy back together again.

Nick didn't do miracles. No psychiatrist did. He would try his best, but he would not feel guilty if his best was not enough for this little boy. He would not beat himself up over what the world had done to this boy or how the boy handled what the world had dealt him. When Nick climbed into bed at night and closed his eyes, he would not see this little boy's face during the seemingly eternal space of time that elapsed before he actually went to sleep.

With effort, Nick made his way into the room where the little boy was resting. He sat down in the desk chair pulled to the side of the bed, leaning his elbows on his knees and his chin on his hands. Before he could say a word, the boy dismissed him by turning his head toward the wall.

At first, Nick tried talking about anything, everything and nothing at all. That got no reaction at all.

How had he done this before? He'd never had trouble making conversation. But everything felt different now. The old instincts he'd trusted for so long had deserted him, and things that used to come to him effortlessly were more of a struggle than he'd imagined.

It felt as if he'd simply lost every bit of knowledge inside his head. How was he supposed to help this child?

Suddenly Nick spotted a textbook on the desk, and he remembered something he'd done once much earlier in his career when he'd felt much the way he was feeling today. He picked up the book and dropped it on the floor beside the bed.

The boy jumped at the noise, turned back around and glared at Nick.

"So, you can hear. That's good." He felt the slightest bit guilty for finding out that way, but if they were going to talk, he had to know the boy could hear him, and the boy had to know that Nick knew. Otherwise this deaf routine could go on forever.

Nick didn't think he was dealing with a child from the streets, not by the way the boy reacted to the noise. He'd nearly jumped out of his skin. He was scared, and he didn't try to hide it from Nick.

A street kid worked hard not to let his fear show.

"Look, I'm sorry," he said. "I didn't mean to frighten you."

The boy gave up nothing.

"Do you have a name? It doesn't have to be your real one, just something I can call you."

The boy just glared at him.

Nick tried everything he could think of to get the boy to talk. Nothing worked. Finally, Nick laid it on the line for the little boy.

"Look," he said. "This is how it is. You can't stay here. You're too young, and A.J. has already called social services. You know what those people will do? They'll take you downtown. They'll fill out all sorts of paperwork and make a million phone calls. Then they'll start looking for someone to take care of you while they find your mother or your father or your grandmother. Believe me, kid, you don't want to go through that unless you absolutely have to. So why don't you just tell me—who can we call to come and get you?"

Again Nick received a blank stare in return. He pulled a pen out of his pocket and a notepad out off the desk.

"How about writing it down, then," he said. At times kids found writing things down less threatening than saying them aloud. "Can you do that for me?"

The boy refused to take the pen.

"I'm trying to help you," Nick said. "I swear I am."

But the kid didn't want his help. Finally, disgusted with himself and thinking that this child deserved someone much more professional and compassionate than he could possibly be, he simply gave up and took the boy downstairs to the party.

An hour and a half later, Nick stood outside the cafeteria, where the party was winding down.

"Excuse me. Do you work here?"

He turned. Standing in the hallway, he saw the figure of a young woman in jeans and a sweater, long black hair streaming down her back. "What can I do for you?"

"I'm looking for a little boy. His name is Rico Leone. Someone at the police station said he might be here."

"Oh," Nick said. "Our mystery man upstairs. Eight or nine years old, skinny, short curly brown hair and brown eyes, light-brown skin?"

"That's him. He's eight." She sounded relieved. "Is he all right?"

Nick wanted to give the young woman hell about losing track of the boy for what they suspected was a couple of days. He felt that old familiar stirring of anger over the way a child had been treated by the people who were supposed to take care of him, and for a moment, he felt more alive than he had in months.

Then, just as quickly as it came, the feeling was gone. He was calm again, cool, unaffected by it all. That brief flickering of emotion simply died within him.

"Well?"

The woman sounded worried when he didn't answer right away.

"Is he all right?"

The flicker was back, stronger than before, but would it be just as fleeting? He thought about the boy huddled in the corner of the shelter. No, he couldn't pass on this, and let loose full force on the woman.

"He was starving, soaked to the skin, shaking from the cold. Other than that, he was fine . . . physically."

"Physically?"

That seemed to frighten her.

"What aren't you telling me?"

"Who are you?" Nick asked, losing his patience with this whole situation. "Are you his mother? Are you the one who lost track of him for the past two or three days?"

The woman flushed hotly. Nick noted with some detachment that her coloring was striking—jet-black hair, a mountain of it, caught up in a thick braid that hung down her back, nearly black eyes fringed with dark, thick lashes.

When was the last time he'd noticed the color of a woman's hair or her eyes?

"If I were his mother, I would not 'lose track' of him for three days at a time. I'm his teacher," she said quite deliberately, as if talking to someone with the IQ of a rock. "You can call me Ms. Sandoval."

Nick took another look. She was petite, fresh faced, with all that hair, those eyes and this beautiful olive skin. The musical lilt to her speech had him wondering about her ancestry. Spanish, he guessed, or maybe Latin American. She caught him staring, and that clearly annoyed her even more.

"Who are *you?*" she asked.

Her tone was one he was sure she used on the kids in her classroom.

A year ago, he would have given his name and identified himself as a doctor. A year ago, half the population of Chicago wouldn't have recognized him and hated him on sight.

"I'm Nick," he said simply.

"Nick?"

"I'm a psychiatrist."

"That explains it," she said.

It explained nothing to Nick, though.

"Could you tell me what's wrong with Rico?"

"It's hard to say. He won't talk to us."

"What do you mean?"

"He hasn't said a word. Not since he showed up here. We had no idea who he was. We were just hoping someone would report him missing and the police would send them here."

"I can't believe he wouldn't have someone call me," the woman said, looking hurt rather than annoyed at him. "And what about his mother? Did he say where his mother is? Does he even know?"

This situation grew only more puzzling to Nick. He wished now that he'd escaped from the shelter when he had the chance. "I have no idea where his mother is, but I would like to know her name."

"Renata Leone." She rattled off an address. "But no one is there. I went there first, but the place had been ... trashed."

"Trashed?"

The woman nodded. "Can I see the boy?"

"Sure. Follow me. He may be asleep, but we can check." Nick led her down the hallway toward the back stairs.

"What's going to happen to him?" she asked.

"It's hard to say. We called Child and Family Services, and we're waiting for someone from their office to show up."

"He'll go into foster care?"

"If they can't locate his mother or a relative."

"Did you tell him that? He must have been so scared, because he hated it there," she said.

"He's been in foster care before?" Nick asked.

"Last year, before he came to live with me for a while."

"With you? I thought you said you were his teacher."

"I am, and for a while I was his foster parent."

"Oh." Nick didn't know many teachers who went to those lengths to help their students.

"His mother...she has her problems."

"Don't we all."

She stopped dead in the middle of the hallway and whirled around. "I can't believe you said that."

"Oh, really?" Apparently, he'd set her off again. He wondered how she managed to teach with that temper of hers.

"You've got some nerve, Doctor."

She made his title sound like a dirty word.

"I know just your type."

"Really?" Nick knew he should put an end to this right now, while she still had no idea who he was.

He knew what would happen once she figured it out. There would be this long silence, this puzzled stare, then a flicker of recognition, morbid curiosity, then most likely anger. Most people had convicted him based on nothing more than what they'd heard on TV about the case.

This woman had judged him inside of two minutes based on something he didn't understand at all. He was curious, and he was mad. He was sick and tired of being found guilty by a bunch of strangers.

"And just what do you know about me and my type?" he asked, going with the anger that he'd kept bottled inside him for so long.

She moved a step closer. "You come down here to the poor side of town, wearing your fancy clothes and your expensive shoes, worrying that someone is going to mess up your car while you're in this lousy neighborhood.

"You give these people a few hours of your time every week or every month, and you think you've done your civic duty. You go home to your fancy apartment on that nice, safe part of town and you don't feel as guilty anymore. And you manage to forget all about these kids."

Under any other circumstances, Nick would have admired her for sticking up for Rico and all the other kids like him.

Any other day—when he hadn't just walked into Hope House for the first time in a year and hadn't been half-scared out of his mind over a fifteen-minute, one-sided conversation with a little boy in trouble—and Nick would have cut her some slack for the way she lit into him.

But not today.

"Lady," he told her, "you're way out of line."

"Am I? I've seen your kind before."

"My kind? You don't even know me."

She just glared at him. Obviously she cared a great deal about the kids with whom she worked.

He wanted to tell her to give it up, that she was only going to get her heart broken again and again, but he doubted she would listen to anything he had to say.

Besides, he was actually enjoying sparring with her. He didn't think he'd had a conversation or an argument with anyone in the past year that he'd enjoyed. He took it one more step. "And I suppose you're going to save the world single-handedly?"

"No, just my little corner of it."

Nick shook his head and struggled to hold his tongue. He had nothing to prove to this woman. Still, he had an urge to tell her just how much of himself he'd given these kids, how much of himself he'd lost and might never regain. He fought that urge and won this time. Let this woman keep her illusions, her naiveté. She would lose them one day, just as he had.

"Up the stairs, down the hall, to your right. It's the second door on the right," he told her tightly. "Once you've seen him, come downstairs and ask for A.J. The two of you can decide what to do with him."

Nick turned and left.

Chapter 2

Laura Sandoval was fuming as she followed that arrogant man's directions. He said he was a psychiatrist. Years ago she had nearly married a psychiatrist. She was afraid Mitch had left her with something of a blind spot. Still, that wasn't the only thing that upset her where this man was concerned.

She was truly sick of the way wealthy people came into these neighborhoods, looking down their noses, shaking their heads and clicking their tongues. Who were they to judge? They always had their safe, secure world to return to. She saw it happen too many times.

Families in these parts could eat for months on what that man downstairs had spent on his shoes. So how could he possibly know anything about these kids or their mothers or their problems?

Laura hoped he hadn't said anything to Rico to upset him. She'd lay into him again if he had.

She was relieved when she found the little boy curled up under the blanket asleep. She leaned over the bed and stared down into that familiar face. Some of the tension of the past few hours started to ease.

Rico. What in the world was he doing all the way across town? And where had he been for the past three days? Surely not on the streets alone. Surely he would have called her rather than stay on the streets. He'd grown up on the North Side of Chicago. He knew how dangerous it was out there.

Laura pulled the desk chair over to the bed and sat beside him for a minute. She put her hand in his hair, ran her thumb through his curls, then wiped away a tear from her cheek.

Rico's mother had been in and out of drug-treatment centers over the past year, and after Rico's first, bewildering experience with foster care, Laura had decided she wouldn't let anyone put him through that again. She became his foster parent, taking him into her home, giving him his own special corner of her heart.

Twice in the past year he'd come to live with her. Twice, with great difficulty, she'd relinquished him to the dubious care of his mother. Could she do that again? Give him up like that?

She wasn't sure. But she knew one thing for certain. She would never turn her back on this child when he needed her help. Not now. Not ever.

Nick was outside in the rain, almost to his car, and he felt like throwing up. How long had it been since he'd felt so powerless? So helpless? So alone?

He turned around and was back inside the shelter. He walked swiftly and purposefully to the back of the building, up the back steps and across the hall to the room where Rico slept.

Nick would not sleep tonight. Cold, wet, hungry, with blood splattered on his shoes—Nick couldn't shake that description out of his mind. What in the world had happened to the boy?

His teacher said the Leones' apartment had been trashed and there was no sign of Rico's mother. Nick suspected fear had kept the boy silent.

What had the boy seen? What kind of danger could he be in because of it? Nick hated to think about that.

He rounded the corner and looked through the doorway. Inside, the woman was stroking the boy's back, making small circles with her splayed fingers.

So, this was her Rico. Nick needed to be sure about that before he left. He wanted assurance that the boy had someone to look out for him. And not just any-one—Rico had a tiger on his side, and she was going to save her little corner of the world.

Nick hoped she managed to do that before some-thing robbed her of her illusions, as he'd been robbed of his.

Still, he couldn't help but look on, fascinated, as the woman comforted the boy. She felt his forehead, checking for a temperature. The boy had none before when Nick checked him.

The woman's touch was filled with almost a rever-ence. Watching her, Nick sensed something stirring inside him, some emotion he couldn't name, some yearning that had been long denied.

The woman lifted the blanket covering the boy and pulled up his shirt, no doubt looking for any sign he'd been hurt. A.J. had already done that and told Nick she'd found no obvious injuries, nothing to account for the blood on his shoes or his clothes.

Only then did Nick remember—he hadn't told the woman about the blood.

He saw her tuck the cover securely around Rico, stroke his hair once more, then wipe away a tear.

Nick wondered just how many tears she'd already shed over this particular child, how many more tears she would cry over him in the future.

He turned away to leave, not wanting to think that at one time he'd shed tears of his own over some lost child.

Behind him, the woman gasped, and Nick brought his attention back to her. She held one of the boy's shoes in her hand. Blood.

Nick must have made some sound, something to alert her to his presence, because she whirled around and faced him. Holding the shoe in her hand and looking at him accusingly, she demanded, "What is going on here?"

Suddenly Rico stirred. Both stared at the boy, who merely turned over and settled back to sleep again.

Nick motioned for the woman to come into the hallway, then closed the door. He was sure they were going to end up arguing again, and he didn't want their discussion to wake up Rico.

"There's blood on his shoes."

"And his pant leg." Nick swallowed hard. He'd had the most peculiar response to blood ever since the shooting. He could get a paper cut with two drops of blood on it and actually feel light-headed—him, a man who'd been through medical school and interned in the emergency room before settling on psychiatry. It was the most ridiculous thing. But this wasn't about him, he reminded himself. This was about Rico.

"You didn't tell me that," the woman accused.

He was tempted to say that she never asked, that he'd barely gotten a word in after she finished trying to take him down a notch or two. But he was too surprised at finding out something he had no business noticing—here in this instant one of the most basic of human emotions—well, male emotions, at least—had come roaring back to life.

He wanted her. A man who for months now had lived like a monk, found himself attracted to this woman.

He couldn't say why it had happened now, with her. Granted, she was attractive, but so were a lot of women he knew. He hadn't had a lustful thought about anyone in—

"What are you doing?" she said.

Nick was caught staring at her breasts. "Damn," he said, staring at her.

"Well?" She demanded an answer.

What could he say? That she had somehow shaken him out of this awful lethargy he'd been trapped in for months, that he'd just discovered there might be some spark of life left in him, after nearly giving himself up for dead?

He wasn't about to tell her those things. And he was having trouble concentrating on anything she was saying anyway. He wanted to know if this was real or if it was some sort of a fluke. Would he go back to his apartment and bury himself alive for the next year? Or was he coming out of this awful fog that had settled around him following the shooting? Could this woman transform him back to the man he was before?''

He doubted it. After all, she thought he was nuts. Hell, until a few hours ago, he wouldn't have argued the point with her.

"I'm sorry," he said, not about to explain why.

She paused for a moment, tilting her head so slightly to one side. She opened her mouth to say something, but didn't. She took a step backward, away from him.

He threw up his hands in front of him to tell her she had nothing to fear from him. He didn't think anything had embarrassed him this much since he was fifteen and trying so clumsily to seduce the girl next door. And he'd give anything if this beautiful woman would somehow forget that the past fifteen seconds had ever happened. She could go back to chewing him out and hating his guts. Contempt, hostility, even rage—those he could handle. This unnameable thing between them was something different altogether.

Nick watched while she squared her shoulders and crossed her arms in front of her, then came at him again.

"What happened to Rico?" she demanded.

Relieved, he said, "I don't know, and he wouldn't tell us.''

"Why?" she asked. "Why wouldn't he say anything to you? And what could have happened to him?''

"I'm sorry. I don't know.''

"He's not hurt, is he?''

Nick felt a flicker of shame for the way he'd treated her. "No, not that we've discovered.''

"The blood isn't his?''

"We didn't find any marks on him. Did you?''

"No." She shook her head. "No one has seen his mother in three days or so."

"Is that unusual? For her to simply disappear and leave him on his own?"

"No, it's not."

Nick swore softly. What kind of a world was this where it wasn't unusual for mothers to go off and leave their children for days at a time?

He knew the answer to that—a crazy one. They lived in a crazy, mixed-up world.

But that wasn't Nick's problem any longer. The boy in the room wasn't, either, though Nick couldn't stop himself from asking, "How long has he been missing from school?"

"Three days." She took a long, shaky breath. "Do you really think he's been on the streets for three days?"

Nick shrugged. "It's impossible to know for sure. Hopefully, when he wakes up, he'll tell you."

She leaned back against the wall and hung her head, for the first time losing that shield of invincibility she wore so well. She looked scared now.

"I can't—" She hesitated.

Amazed, Nick realized they'd spoken several civil sentences in a row to each other.

In another lifetime, Nick would have smiled at her. He'd been told women liked his smile. He would have admired her, too. They would have shared a common goal—looking out for kids like the one on the bed in A.J.'s old room. And maybe they would have been friends, maybe something more.

In another lifetime.

But not now.

"You can't...what?" he asked in his best professionally detached manner.

She looked at him sharply. If she was going to analyze him, he wished her luck. He was doing a miserable job of it himself, and he was trained for it.

"I can't believe he didn't come to me," she said. "Or at least phone me. He has my number. I made him memorize it. And he knows he can call me anytime."

"He's lucky to have someone like you," Nick said, and meant it. Again he felt her gaze on him, as she measured him and his words. "I'm not such a rotten guy," he felt compelled to add.

"I didn't say that you were."

"Not exactly," he said, then found himself smiling in spite of himself. Maybe he could dazzle her just a little with one of his smiles.

Nick could have left right then, but he stayed. He told himself he was simply making conversation when he said, "Tell me about Rico and his mother and this apartment that's been trashed."

Laura took a minute to think about whether she wanted to comply. And she was still in shock over how good this man looked with a smile on his face. Not that she was the kind of woman to be bowled over by an attractive man. Mitch Davis had cured her of that long ago.

But the transformation of Nick's face was incredible. What was once forbidding had become inviting. What she'd taken initially for sheer arrogance had become a cocky self-assuredness not without its charm. And the smile, coupled with his easy manner in which he showed her that her near insult hadn't wounded him at all, told her his ego wasn't as big as she feared at first.

Maybe this man would prove to be tolerable after all.

Laura was disconcerted to realize that now she was the one staring so blatantly at him, and she quickly forced herself to look away.

What had he said? He wanted to know about Rico and his mother. Because he truly cared? Or because he was simply making conversation? She would have to find out.

"So," he said, "you go out looking for all your students when they miss class?"

She was about to deny it, but the truth was, she didn't let any student miss class for an extended period of time without finding out why. "Someone has to watch out for them."

"And you're the guardian angel of the—what grade is he in?"

Laura certainly didn't feel like an angel around this man. "Second grade, at Saint Anne's."

Nick whistled. "Rough neighborhood. And he's a long way from home."

"I know."

"So what happened?"

Again she wondered whether his concern was genuine. Laura still cared deeply for all her students. She had little patience for people who worked with children yet didn't care.

Today had been a particularly hard day for her because she had said goodbye to her students for the summer. She could still see them huddled around her, twenty-two pairs of arms trying to reach her, tugging at her from all directions, as the kids tried to make the final few moments of the school year last a little longer.

Laura's kids weren't the kind to count the days until the end of the term because they wanted out of school. For her students, school was often their haven, away from the noise, the overcrowding, the ugliness and the violence. Most of them lived with the very real threat of violence every day of their lives in their own neighborhoods.

Her students always found their own special places in her heart.

Everyone told her not to become so involved with them. Other people warned the kids needed too much. That they needed more than one person could possibly give. That she would only end up getting her heart broken in the process. But she wasn't capable of stopping herself. Someone had to help them. Someone had to care and to fight for them. She would quit teaching the day she didn't think she could make a difference.

She wondered why Nick had given up on all these kids around him. Somehow she felt certain he had. And that puzzled her, now that she decided she might have judged him too hastily.

He was still waiting for her answer, and Laura decided he deserved one.

"Today was the last day of school," she began. "It was the third day in a row Rico missed, and I knew there was no way he would miss the last day of school unless something was wrong. So I went to look for him. When I knocked on the door to the apartment, the door wasn't even shut, so I walked in."

Laura hadn't prepared herself for anything like the scene in front of her. The apartment wasn't simply dirty or messy—it had been trashed. Everything inside had been pulled out of place, turned over, broken, with piles of rubble left in the middle of the floor.

"They were searching for something," Laura said. "Thoroughly and recklessly searching. They didn't care who knew it."

"Who?" Nick said. "And searching for what?"

"I don't know."

"Does his mother do drugs?"

Laura nodded. "She's been in and out of drug treatment centers all year."

"Maybe she crossed someone. Maybe one of her suppliers?"

Laura had considered the possibility. The sad part was that it probably didn't really matter what Renata was doing to endanger Rico. Simply living in parts of Chicago was a hazard to the children. In some neighborhoods, kids were killed in their own living rooms or on their way to school just because they were in the line of fire when someone started shooting.

It was absolutely insane.

"So," Nick said, "you didn't find out anything at the apartment?"

She shook her head. "I walked through the place, to make sure they weren't...there." She couldn't bring herself to put into words what she had feared finding in that apartment.

"Lady, you need a keeper. Do you have some kind of death wish or something?"

"I had an eight-year-old boy who was missing."

Nick's look told her he didn't think that justified her actions in the least.

"They're just little kids," she insisted. "Someone has to look out for them. You can't tell me that doesn't matter to you at all."

Laura knew she must have hit some nerve with him because she saw his whole face change. It looked as if a mask had slid down over his features, blocking out all the light and the warmth, leaving the cold, hard stranger from downstairs in their place. It was chilling to see a man change so quickly and so completely.

"Go ahead," he said, appearing totally disinterested. "Tell me the rest of it."

"Then I started knocking on their neighbors' doors until someone answered. An elderly woman finally admitted that she hadn't seen Rico or his mother in three days and she was worried about them. Two nights ago, she heard what sounded like someone tearing apart their apartment."

"Did you call the police?"

"I went to the station and filled out a missing persons report on both of them, but once I told the officer Renata just disappears from time to time, he wasn't that interested."

Laura remembered now that Rico's mother used to date a policeman, though she couldn't recall his name. Maybe if she did, she could go to that officer for help.

"How did you find us?" Nick asked.

"I was getting ready to leave, when one of the officers at the front desk got a bulletin saying a little boy fitting Rico's description had been found here. It was hard to believe he would come all this way by himself, but that was the only lead I had. So I came here hoping to find him."

And found this enigmatic man, as well. Now that she'd found him, what was she going to do with him?

Laura could put up with him if he actually could help Rico. She could put up with anybody who would help Rico. Still, the idea of spending time with this man, of entrusting Rico into his care, was terribly unsettling.

However, there was really no choice. For the past year, Rico had been the troubled kid in her classroom whom Laura had most wanted to save, the one who broke her heart day after day with his spirit, his trials and tribulations, his hopes.

She had hope for Rico. He could be saved. And Laura Sandoval was going to fight for him. She would put up with the devil himself if she thought he could help Rico.

Chapter 3

To Nick's relief, A.J. came around the corner a minute later with a woman he recognized as a social worker. Nick saw his chance to escape, and he took it. In the flurry of introductions that followed, he slipped out the door. He was halfway down the back stairs, when A.J. caught up with him.

"Gotcha." She looked pleased with herself. "You're just not as fast as you used to be. Now you're going to have to talk to me."

Nick swore softly under his breath. It seems he'd traded one thoroughly unsettling woman for another. Resigned to the fact that he wouldn't get away without saying something, he turned to face A.J.

They hadn't had time to talk before, and he could just imagine what she wanted to talk about. Nick didn't want to hear what she thought of the way he was living right now, or what a wonderful step she thought he'd taken in coming down there tonight.

So, if A.J. was determined to talk, they would have to talk about her. He needed to let her know that he'd accepted what had happened and that he wanted her to be happy. Jack MacAlister had damned well better make her happy.

Nick couldn't deny that she looked great, even if she was pregnant with another man's child. "I saw the pink ribbons all over the place," Nick said. "So I guess..."

"It's a girl."

"I'm happy for you, A.J." It amazed him how far she'd come in such a short time. She used to run this shelter. And at one time, she was one of the kids who'd walked in off the streets into another runaway shelter in this city, one where Nick happened to be working.

Until about eighteen months ago, A.J. had had no idea what her life had been like before she was thirteen. Nick had helped reunite A.J. with her family, and lost her to another man in the process. He would never forget her. And he had the urge to tell her, just in case she didn't already know, how proud he was of her for what she'd made of her life.

"You look beautiful," he said, settling for that to start.

Her hair was a little longer, enough to cover her ears now. She'd gained a little weight—something she badly needed to do. And with the baby... He wasn't sure he could explain it. She looked outrageously radiant now, despite all she'd been through.

A.J. stepped back. "I don't think I ever got over being mad at you long enough to tell you I'll always be grateful for what you did last year. I don't think anyone but you would have made the connection between me and that old picture of Annie."

A.J. still spoke of Annie McKay as if she were someone else, and in many ways Annie was. A.J. was a different person now.

"You do look beautiful," he repeated, because he knew she had a hard time seeing herself that way, and because a part of him would always love her.

He thought for a minute she was going to cry, then she quipped, "You look like hell, Nick."

He nodded and tried to smile. He knew he looked bad, just as he knew she was worried about him. She would help him, if only he would let her.

"I have to go."

He thought she might argue for a minute. She knew he had absolutely no obligations, nothing that meant he had to leave here at any certain time for any purpose. She took another step back. "And I need to get in there and find out about our mystery man. Thanks for coming tonight."

He shrugged. "I didn't do anything."

"Yes, you did."

Laura knew all about social workers and paperwork and the bureaucracy of the social-services system; she'd been through this routine before, which made the process relatively easy this time around.

There were never enough spaces in foster care for the kids who needed help, so Sharon Sawyer was relieved to know she wouldn't have to spend the night on the phone trying to find someone who could take Rico on a temporary basis.

All the social worker had to do was check to make sure Laura's paperwork was in order from the last time she served as a foster parent for Rico, process another mountain of paperwork and turn the boy over to Laura.

Since it was already after ten and Rico was asleep, Sharon agreed to let Rico stay put until morning, when they could hopefully sort this whole thing out.

There was also the matter of finding Rico's mother, but Laura was going to leave that to the social worker and the police. Her concern was with Rico.

She leaned against the doorway to Rico's room. A.J. had returned, and she was now saying a lengthy goodbye to Sharon.

"Sorry," A.J. said, turning back to Laura now that the social worker was leaving. "It's my last day on the job, and I'm not sure when I'll see Sharon again."

Laura couldn't help but notice that A.J. was pregnant and from what she'd seen, the kids and the staff at the shelter adored her. Laura felt a bit envious, particularly of the child she carried.

"You're taking some time off until after the baby comes?" she asked.

"I'm not sure yet. If my husband had his way, I'd never set foot in this part of town again, but he knows how I feel about the kids, so . . . we're going to have to do some talking."

Her smile said it all. Laura bet this woman could talk her husband into anything she wanted.

"So?" A.J. looked around. "Nick didn't get anything out of this little guy. That's too bad."

"You . . . know Nick well?" Laura asked. That seemed to be the safest question of all.

A.J. nodded. "And I think I let him get away much too easily just now. Let's see if we can catch him before he leaves."

Laura followed A.J. down the stairs. "If you wouldn't mind, and if there's room, do you think I could stay the night?"

"Of course," A.J. said, as if it never occurred to her that Laura would stay anywhere else while Rico was here.

"I'd hate for Rico to wake up and be alone," Laura said.

"We'll make Nick carry a cot upstairs for you."

Laura smiled, liking the idea of this woman enlisting the help of the psychiatrist with the fancy shoes for manual labor. "Is he…?" How ever could she phrase this? "Is he always so…?"

A.J. didn't beat around the bush at all, and if anything she seemed a bit protective.

"I heard the two of you got into it in the hallway downstairs."

Laura felt a sliver of what could only be described as shame. Normally, she tried to give everyone the benefit of the doubt. She hadn't been that generous with the man downstairs.

"Nick has been through a rough time," A.J. continued. "But he's definitely one of the good guys. He's the best, in fact. Do me a favor. Cut him some slack, okay? He's not exactly himself today."

Laura waited for her to elaborate. What exactly was he like normally? What kind of a rough time had he gone through? Had he dented his BMW? Gotten mud on those fancy shoes of his? Somehow she knew that wasn't what A.J. was talking about. Still, he was well educated, and he obviously had a lot of money. She would bet he'd had every advantage from the time he was born. How difficult could his problems be compared with those of someone like Rico Leone?

Laura was ashamed of herself then. It was unkind of her to think like that, and she wasn't an unkind person. But she was having a very bad day.

Laura was so worried about Rico. She couldn't imagine him surviving on the streets alone. His apartment had been trashed. His mother was gone. And the blood . . .

What in the world did that mean? How did it fit into this whole mess? She wasn't sure she wanted to know, but feared she was going to find out.

Nick would just have to take care of his own problems.

They didn't find the good doctor anywhere inside the shelter, but they did find A.J.'s husband, who carried the cot upstairs for Laura. Then he escorted his wife out of the shelter after she'd hugged all the kids, cried over them, threatened many of them if they didn't straighten up, then cried all over them again.

Laura stood there and watched it all, thinking that A.J. was a person she could admire and that maybe she had been unkind to the doctor.

Now she stood outside the entrance to the shelter amid the twinkling white lights that had so intrigued her when she'd arrived. Laura looked at her watch and saw that it was nearly eleven now. She had a cot upstairs and A.J.'s promise that the staff would let her spend the night. She was tired, but too keyed up to sleep.

Her car was parked across the street and just down the block, and she had her grade book and a ton of other paperwork to finish before she was done for the school year. If she couldn't sleep, she might as well get some work done. That way, she'd be free to concentrate on Rico tomorrow. She had a feeling the next few days were going to be hectic.

She glanced at the street, hearing the roar of cars and horns and laughter nearby but seeing no activity in the immediate vicinity. The rain was still falling, a surprisingly cold rain for late May. It was only a block, she told herself, then went dashing across the pavement.

A man stepped out of the shadows of the deserted building across from the shelter when she was nearly to the curb. She had this impression of blackness, of imposing height, broad shoulders and strength.

She stumbled to a halt, her momentum nearly sending her toppling forward, then covered her hand with her mouth as she tried not to panic. The shelter was just across the street, she told herself, glancing back and seeing the reassuring glow of the blinking white lights. There was someone watching the door all night. All she had to do was yell, and the man at the shelter would hear her.

Just as she opened her mouth to scream, the man in front of her took one more step, bringing himself out of the shadows, and she could see him clearly now.

"Nick." The word came out on a sigh of relief, relief that was short-lived. She really didn't know anything about this man, except that A.J. liked him. Standing there alone with him in the darkness of the deserted street didn't do much to reassure her.

He said something she didn't hear right away because of some noise nearby. All she knew was that he was reaching for her. He grabbed her by the arms and pulled her to him before she could cry out.

She fought him, pulling herself back with as much force as she could muster. She thought about kicking at his shins or getting her knee up higher to do some real damage, and then she felt the water slamming against feet and her ankles, felt the whish of air at her back, turned and saw taillights glowing through the blackness and the rain.

A car. She'd been standing in the street in the rain when a car had come by. Laura felt so foolish. He was trying to save her skin, and she'd attacked him like a wild thing. He let go of her now and stepped back, giving her space, then time to reflect on how foolishly she'd reacted.

"I didn't even see the car," she said.

He didn't say anything, but he looked...angry would be her first guess, but she wasn't sure that was right. Why would he be angry because she'd overreacted?

Then he laughed bleakly, sarcastically, a sound that nearly made her heart ache it was so lonely, so hopeless.

"I sank to a new low tonight," he said. "Scaring innocent women on the street corner."

"I didn't know it was you," she said, thinking that wasn't totally a lie. She hadn't recognized him at first. "I'm sorry. I hope I didn't hurt you."

She saw his lips twitch, again had that impression of strength and height and power. Still, he didn't give in to what she was sure was the urge to scoff at her and her ability to cause any real harm to someone his size.

"What are you doing out here in the middle of the night by yourself?" he asked.

He sounded as if he had a perfect right to inquire, as if she were some helpless little woman without a hint of a brain in her head.

Laura squared her shoulders, drawing herself up as tall as she could manage at five-four. "I could have you lying on your back on the pavement in three seconds flat," she boasted.

He whistled, mocking her with the sound. "I might just have to see that to believe it."

Laura almost wished he'd give her the chance.

"Even if you think you could throw me," Nick said, "surely you know it's foolish to risk walking around out here at night by yourself."

"You're here," she felt compelled to remind him, but couldn't stop wondering what in the world he was doing out in the street.

It was raining, cold, dark, dangerous. And she'd already decided he was only at the shelter to ease his conscience. So why would he be standing around in the rain like this?

Laura wished she could fit him into some neat little peg, some preconceived notion she had about men like him, but she was starting to see that he wasn't going to make it that easy on her.

"Why are you here, Dr.—"

"Garrett," he supplied, then waited. "Dr. Nicholas Garrett."

Dr. Nicholas Garrett. Was the name supposed to mean something to her? It was vaguely familiar, though she couldn't place it. She let herself look him over leisurely now, maybe even mockingly, because he'd certainly taken his time looking her over this evening. He was a full head taller than she was, and she remembered all too clearly the steely strength of his arms.

He had dark, thick, beautifully textured hair, pushed back from his forehead in luxurious waves. His eyes were smoky black, his brows and lashes the same, and she couldn't say what it was exactly about his face that she found so expressive, so compelling, yet almost... bleak was what came first to her mind.

A.J. had said he'd been through a rough time lately, and now that she was looking for evidence of that, Laura saw it easily in that hauntingly beautiful face of his.

It made her think of the devil before he'd fallen from grace. She could just imagine Satan himself looking as compelling, as fearsome and as handsome as Dr. Nicholas Garrett.

Laura broke out from under that spell of his. "Well, Dr. Garrett—"

"I think we can make it 'Nick,' all things considered," he said.

"Nick," she said, as still he watched her much too intently for her own comfort. "I'm going to get some things out of my car, and then I'm going back to the shelter to spend the night so I can be there when Rico wakes up in the morning."

She couldn't say why she had told him. It certainly wasn't any of his business where she went or where she spent the night. But she felt compelled to say something and to get away from him. An explanation seemed to fill the bill perfectly.

He didn't respond. Exasperated, tired and hating to leave Rico alone any longer, she turned and headed for the car.

"Wait a minute," he said, coming up behind her. "I'll walk you over."

"It's not necessary."

"Indulge me on this," he said, putting his hand at the back of her waist and falling into step with her. "Unless you are afraid of me."

Something—more the tone of his voice than the actual words—stopped her cold in her tracks. Was she afraid of him? She was fooling herself in thinking he wouldn't pick up on her uneasiness.

"You just startled me, that's all." She felt a sudden urge to reassure him.

He reminded her of someone, some lost little boy. She smiled, unable to help herself when she imagined what he'd think if he ever knew she was comparing him to one of her students. They got lost sometimes, basically good kids who for one reason or another just lost all sense of themselves and the things that were important. And that was the most dangerous kind of all. The kids who didn't care about themselves were the ones who made disastrous mistakes with their lives, sometimes mistakes that couldn't ever be corrected.

Rico wasn't one of those kids. The world he lived in might have gone mad, but he still believed in himself. Laura had a hunch Dr. Nicholas Garrett couldn't say the same for himself. Then she remembered A.J.'s comment.

Exactly how did one go about cutting some slack to a dangerously handsome man who reminded her alternately of the devil and a lost little boy?

Laura was certain she didn't need to find out. She collected deprived kids the way some people picked up stray cats and took them home with them; she certainly couldn't start treating grown men the same way. Although, for a second, the thought of taking him home had her heart kicking into high gear.

Here he was, standing in the rain beside her, the tension between the two of them a palpable thing now. He wanted something from her. He needed it. But what was it? And did she have it to give?

"I'm not afraid of you, Nick," she said as calmly and as evenly as possible.

Then she started toward her car. He matched her stride step for step down the deserted street, waited while she unloaded a tote bag from the car and, without a word, walked her back to the shelter. They stood in the entranceway, just out of the rain, the man at the door looking pointedly in the other direction. Laura felt as awkward as a teenager coming home from her first date, except she'd never dated a man like Nick.

Who was she kidding? She had hardly dated at all. There were no parents, no family home, and she hated explaining her foster parents to a high-school boy. So she hadn't explained, and she hadn't dated.

Now she wondered whether this moment would have been any easier if she'd been more experienced talking to a man she hardly knew.

Surely it had to get easier than this.

"I hope things work out... for Rico," he said, facing her now with a foot and a half between them.

Laura swallowed hard, wondering why her throat would be so tight and why she had to struggle to control her breathing, wondering what in the world was happening between her and this man.

She thought about asking him to explain it; after all, he was the one with the medical degree and the specialty in human behavior. She would bet he'd stood on dozens of porches after dozens of dates with women much more self-assured and experienced than her. Surely he knew just what to do.

But asking him to explain those things would put more importance on this moment than it truly deserved.

After all, nothing had happened. He'd sparred with her in the hallway of the shelter, caught her against him for the briefest moment of time while the car whizzed past, walked her to her car.

It didn't mean anything at all.

"I'm not such a bad guy," he said again, bringing a smile to her lips. "And I just realized—I don't know your first name."

She flushed profusely. She had been downright rude to him. Working up her courage, she extended an unsteady hand toward him. "It's Laura."

He took her hand in his—enveloped it in both of his, actually. She gave a little start as his hands closed around hers. His skin was impossibly warm for a cold, wet night like this, and she couldn't help but think that if it felt this good simply to hold his hand, how would it feel to be in his arms?

It was a silly thought, a girlish one. Girls were the ones who stood on the front porch daydreaming about whether they would get a good-night kiss and where things might go from there.

"Laura," he said.

The sound of her name on his lips sent shivers down her spine. Curiously, she felt she would remember this moment forever.

"I have to go," she said, pulling her hand from his before she blurted out any of the ridiculous things she was feeling. And then she disappeared inside the shelter.

She didn't allow herself to look back, not for a second.

Chapter 4

Nick was still thinking about Laura the next morning. Hell, he'd thought about her most of the night.

He seldom slept anymore. And it was much more pleasant to think of Laura than the problems that normally ran through his head.

More frightening, yet just as compelling, were his thoughts of Rico. He hadn't gotten anything out of the kid except a bad case of nerves for himself, and he knew if the kid needed help Laura and A.J. would find someone to help Rico. A.J. wouldn't let a little thing like the fact that she no longer worked at the shelter stop her. He had a feeling Laura Sandoval wouldn't let anything stop her when it came to helping Rico, either.

So the boy wasn't Nick's problem, and Rico would certainly be better off in some other doctor's care. There was only one thing wrong—he couldn't stop thinking about Rico, just as he couldn't stop thinking about Laura.

His apartment, for so long a haven, suddenly seemed to be closing in on him. It was dark here, dusty, dirty. He hadn't been bothered by any of those things before, but now he was. Giving in to the need to do something, to change something, he cleaned up the place. When he finished, he still wasn't tired.

Outside, the rain had washed things fairly clean, at least for a city. The sun was shining, the wind blowing, the sky this intriguing shade of blue. How long had it been since he'd even noticed the color of the sky? Or the state of the weather? Or cared whether it was night or day?

It was still early. What could he do with this day? He went out and simply started walking, amazed to find himself bothered by having nothing to do, no place to be, no obligations to meet. For the longest time, he'd been quite satisfied to live that way. Not today. He didn't even want to think about what this uncharacteristic restlessness meant.

His days used to be crammed full. He'd worked for peanuts for the prosecutors at the federal, state and local levels, testifying in court when they needed an expert witness in psychiatry. He'd also helped in preparing children to testify in court, even helped the authorities in questioning children either victimized by crime or those who'd witnessed violent crimes. That was how he came to work the kidnapping case that eventually brought A.J.'s family back to her.

But Nick had made his money in this fancy office downtown, charging rich people exorbitant rates to try to straighten out their mixed-up kids. And that's where he'd run into trouble last year. Nick, one troubled kid and one innocent bystander who happened to be a teenager himself. That's when Nick fell apart.

Nick hadn't done much of anything since. He still had the right to practice his chosen profession, thanks to the licensing board that reviewed the complaint against him and later cleared him of any wrongdoing. Of course, that board couldn't give him back his privacy, his reputation, the respect of his peers; he'd been crucified in the press for most of the past year. He couldn't imagine parents wanting to bring their children to him for help ever again.

The board's ruling had also done nothing to clear his conscience. He had to do that for himself. Or he had to at least learn to live with what had happened.

So far, he hadn't done either. He'd simply existed in this void inside his apartment, until he'd been drawn back into the real world by one lost little boy and the spitfire of a woman who was determined to help him.

Nick found himself headed for the nearest train station. Within twenty minutes, he was at the shelter, standing in the shadows of the abandoned building across the street, trying to figure out what he was going to say to Laura Sandoval and Rico Leone this time.

Nick wanted to do something. He wanted to help Rico, and he wanted to see Laura in the bright light of day. Surely she wasn't nearly as intriguing as he remembered.

A couple of kids he remembered, kids who hadn't been at A.J.'s party the night before, went inside, and Nick wondered what had happened to them in the past. He could find out. He could walk back in there and ask them. He knew Joe Dailey, the interim director, wouldn't give him any trouble about hanging out there and talking to the kids.

With luck, Joe wouldn't try to talk to Nick about what had happened last year. He would probably ask when Nick was planning to come back to work, but Nick could handle that. He'd give him some offhand nonanswer, and that would be the end of it. Joe wouldn't press him on the issue.

Nick took one long, deep breath and resigned himself to going inside, all the while telling himself it wouldn't mean that much if he did. It was simply what he chose to do with this particular day. No commitments involved.

He almost always made headway with his patients with the idea of taking one day at a time. They didn't have to settle their future that instant. They only had to worry about that day. If they could handle that day, they could probably get through the one after it. And the next one, and the next one. Pretty soon the future would take care of itself, despite their state of uncertainty and self-doubt.

Surely that theory would work with Nick, as well.

He glanced to his left, then his right, found the street empty, and walked across. Some sort of commotion at the shelter entrance—a shout, the pounding of feet—drew his attention. He saw a little boy—Rico—shoot out the doors, down the steps and into the street.

Only then did Nick notice the car. It came barreling out of nowhere, its engine roaring menacingly. And it was headed straight for Rico.

Nick screamed a warning he knew would be too late, and then he, too, was running into the street and into the path of the oncoming car.

Rico stood frozen in place, his mouth gaping but no sound coming out.

Nick grabbed him on the run and lunged for the other side of the street. . . .

Laura shoved open the shelter door just in time to see a man and a little boy flying eerily through the air. She saw it through this curious fog, watched it with this stunned sense of disbelief.

She was dreaming, she told herself. No, she thought—this was a nightmare.

She heard the sickening thud of bodies hitting something—she couldn't see what.

She heard the car engine roaring. The vehicle never even slowed down. People were screaming and had gathered at the entrance to the shelter.

For a moment, Laura couldn't move. She couldn't look. Her stomach churned. She leaned weakly against the side of the building for three or four seconds, then forced herself to move.

Laura pushed through the crowd, to the little boy lying on the sidewalk and a man on his hands and knees, his head bent forward as he gasped for breath.

Rico. There was blood running down the boy's face from a gash on his forehead, fresh scrape marks on his nose and his cheeks. She knelt beside him, afraid to touch him. He was on his side, his eyes closed, his arms outstretched toward her.

Laura's eyes filled with tears.

She was just about to pull him to her, when a man's voice broke through the haze that had settled in around her.

"Don't pick him up," the voice commanded.

She sat back on her heels and turned toward the voice. "Nick?"

He, too, sat back on his heels, breathing heavily, looking as dazed as she felt.

"Don't try to move him," he said, then gasped again.

Torn, she gazed at the little boy and knew she should listen to his advice. She'd been taught enough first aid to know she shouldn't move an accident victim, but she'd never imagined how hard it would be to leave an injured person, especially an injured child, where he had landed.

"Somebody call 911." Nick yelled into the crowd.

"Got it," a voice shouted back.

Laura didn't try to pick up Rico, but she moved as close as she could to him. She called his name softly, then louder.

Nick put a hand on the boy's chest. Laura was relieved to notice that it was still rising and falling; he was breathing.

"Let me in here, Laura," he said.

She hesitated, stricken. She knew what she should do, but she couldn't seem to make herself respond. And she didn't want to leave Rico's side.

"Laura?" he said again, louder this time. "I'm a doctor, remember? Let me try to help him."

Of course. He was a doctor. Psychiatry was a medical specialty. He had a medical degree. He could help. Oh, please, God, let him be able to help.

She moved out of the way and let Nick do what he could.

Rico would be all right, she told herself. He had to be all right.

She repeated that to herself over and over again. Still, it didn't lessen the terror. Every time she closed her eyes, she heard him scream and saw him go flying through the air.

It seemed to take forever for the ambulance to get to the hospital and then for anyone to come out and tell her anything once they reached the ER.

She imagined the worst of things with each passing minute. And she hated hospitals.

When she was eleven, her father was diagnosed with cancer, and so began a seemingly endless string of visits to the hospital. Two exhausting years later, her father was gone. Six months after that, her mother died from a heart attack.

Suddenly Laura was on her own. Her mother's sister had taken her in for a while, then her mother's brother. But no one really had room for her. They all had big families of their own, and there was never enough money to feed and clothe their own children, let alone Laura. After her uncle deserted his wife, Laura was put into the foster-care system; she was fourteen years old.

Laura supposed that was why she didn't think she could ever give too much of herself to the children in her classroom. They were her family. To many of them, she was their anchor.

The only problem was, the children couldn't fill every need a grown woman had. Laura still felt incredibly lonely at times. There was no man in her life; there hadn't been for a very long time. She'd tried to fool herself into believing the children were enough and she didn't need anyone else in her life.

But right now, back in a hospital for the first time in years, she wished someone were there for her.

With that, her thoughts turned to Nick.

She'd somehow lost track of him after they'd gotten to the hospital. She remembered him sliding into the ambulance beside her, consulting with the paramedics and taking her hand in his for a tight, quick squeeze. But as soon as they arrived Nick was gone. He and Rico were now somewhere inside the bedlam of the emergency room. And she was alone again.

Laura looked at her watch—twelve-forty—then tried to remember when this whole nightmare had begun. She paced the floors, gazed out the windows, glanced at the weather report on that all-news channel on the television in the corner.

The woman at the admissions desk didn't have any information for her. Laura tried to look through the doors, to spot which room Rico had been taken into, but didn't see him anywhere. She tried not to think about what that might mean.

People had warned her she had to find a way to harden her heart against everything she saw and heard—otherwise she'd never be able to continue teaching.

But Laura couldn't do that. She was a teacher. If her students needed mothering, she mothered. If they needed a good dressing-down, she delivered it. If they just needed one constant in their lives, one person who would always be there, always care, always listen, she offered them that.

She gave them everything she had to give, every minute, every day, year after year. And it was true, she did get tired. She grew discouraged, at times depressed, often angry. But she'd never give up teaching. She'd sooner cut off her right arm.

But then, it had never been as bad as this. Nothing had hurt her as much as this.

She closed her eyes and offered another heartfelt plea for Rico's recovery.

Sometime later, she was standing in the corner, her back to the room, slowly going out of her mind, when someone touched her lightly on the shoulder.

"Laura?"

She whirled around. "Nick."

He had a white bandage on his right temple, which stood out starkly against his skin and his dark hair; a mean-looking cut at the upper right corner of his lips; and a bruise on his right cheekbone. Confused, Laura touched her fingertips to his cheek, then outlined his lips.

He was real. His skin, rubbed raw in one spot, was still warm to the touch.

And he was back. She was so grateful he was back. She thought she'd only imagined what a lifeline it was to have his hand wrapped around hers for a while on the nightmarish trip to the hospital. But she hadn't. He was standing by her side now, and she had her hand on his face, and she was so thankful for that simple connection between the two of them.

Conscious now of the way she was touching him, she let her hand fall away. And then she realized exactly what she was seeing—what she hadn't seen before on the street when everything had been so crazy.

"It was you?" she asked. "I saw two people go flying through the air. A man and a little boy. And the man was you. Someone told me that a man saved Rico from the worst of the impact, and it was you. You knocked him out of the way of that car."

He merely nodded, eyed her curiously, then caught her by the arms. "You look like you're about to fall over."

She didn't try to deny it. "I didn't know," she said, remembering him gasping on the street beside her. He must have had the wind knocked out him, in addition to everything else. This cut under the bandage, the split lip, the bruise on his face. How had she missed all that? "After it happened, all I could see was Rico. He was the only one I even thought about."

She realized then that he hadn't told her anything about Rico's condition.

"Nick?" she said, more urgently than before.

"He's going to be fine."

She swayed on her feet, but stayed upright thanks to him.

"He has a slight concussion," Nick continued, "some bruises, some scrapes, but so far nothing else."

"So far?"

"They're still checking him over, but I honestly don't think they're going to find anything, Laura. We were nearly to the other side of the street when the car hit us."

"Nearly?" She thought about explaining to him how it had looked from where she stood.

"It just clipped us," he said.

Clipped? He was talking about a car. They'd been run down by a car, for God's sake.

Laura caught her breath at last. She felt his hands holding fast to her arms just above the elbows, gazed up into that darkly handsome face of his, all battered and bruised now. He looked even more appealing than before.

She thought again about fallen angels and devilishly attractive men. How could the two images possibly belong together in one person's face?

"Are you okay?" he asked.

She laughed, the sound warning her how little self-control she had left.

"Laura?"

She forced herself to bring her mind back to the conversation. What were they talking about? Rico. "He's going to be okay?"

Nick nodded.

"And you?" She brought her hand to the side of his face once more. And somehow, when she laid it against his face it felt more like a caress than anything else. "You're all right?"

He nodded, looking as wary as she felt. He still held her by the arms; she still had a hand to his face. And it wasn't enough. She felt herself pulled closer to him by a force she couldn't begin to explain.

Suddenly he pushed her back. "Don't," he said, his hands locked on her arms.

"What?" She didn't understand this at all.

"Don't look at me that way."

He sounded thoroughly disgusted with her and the whole situation, so different from the man who'd held her hand in the ambulance and promised her Rico was going to be fine.

How did he do that? Turn off and on like that? Right now, he looked like that arrogant man with the expensive shoes who had infuriated her in the hallway of the shelter last night. And he looked as though he didn't care about anyone or anything in this world.

"What way?"

"Like I'm going to charge in here on a white horse and make everything better. I'm nobody's savior, Laura," he said bitterly.

Nobody's savior? An odd choice of words. Most definitely, he had saved Rico. She considered pointing that out to him, but didn't think this was the time or the place. She didn't think he would listen and was certain he wouldn't believe her.

"Who are you?" she asked, instead.

"It doesn't matter," he said bleakly, then dropped his hands and walked away.

But it did matter—to Laura at least. It mattered very much. And she had an overwhelming urge to go after him before he disappeared around the corner.

But she stayed put. Rico was somewhere in the emergency room, and she wouldn't leave him.

Still, she didn't want Nick to go either.

Nobody's savior, he'd told her bitterly. What in the world had he meant by that?

Chapter 5

Laura would bet her next month's rent that Nick was coming back. She didn't even question the fact that it was very important to her that he come back.

When she finally got word from one of the nurses about where Rico had been taken, she hurried to the elevators. Walking down the corridor, she found the room easily. Rico was lying on the bed, with an IV in one arm, a blood-pressure cuff on the other and a bandage almost identical to Nick's on his forehead.

As she had the night before, she nervously checked for any other signs of injury, and found none. The nurse promised that the doctor would be in shortly to tell her what was wrong, and she waited impatiently for him.

Laura sat by Rico's side and held his hand, thinking about all they'd been through in less than twenty-four hours... and about Nick.

Thirty minutes later, Nick was back, standing in the doorway to Rico's room. He didn't say anything about where he'd been and seemed determined to pretend nothing had happened between them in the hallway.

Maybe he could forget, or maybe he was good enough at hiding his emotions that he hoped to make her think he'd forgotten. It only served to heighten her curiosity about him even more.

"How is he?" Nick asked at last, still standing in the doorway.

"I don't know. I haven't talked to the doctor yet."

"I could go find someone for you," he offered.

"No." She wasn't going to let him escape that easily, not when she sensed so clearly his need to simply get away—despite the fact that he'd just come back. What was going on here? What was haunting this enigmatic man?

"Are you sure?"

She nodded. "The doctor was called back to the emergency room. The nurse said he should be finished there soon."

"I was downstairs, almost out the door, when I started wondering about something, and I couldn't leave until I knew what happened earlier," Nick explained.

So, he had almost left. Laura couldn't say exactly how that made her feel. But for now, she didn't have to examine those feelings too closely. "What do you mean, what happened earlier?"

"With Rico. Why was he running into the street like that?"

"I don't know." She'd wondered briefly about that herself, when she could force her mind away from the question of whether he was going to be all right.

"What happened inside the shelter this morning?" Nick asked. "Were you with him?"

"Yes."

"Right before it happened?"

"Yes. He was frightened because you and A.J. talked to him about foster care, and he was afraid of going back there. But once he saw me, and once I told him he was going to come home with me, he was . . ."

"What?"

She shook her head. "I was going to say that he was better, but he was still scared."

"Why?"

"I don't know."

"You said he was in foster care before. Did anything happen to him while he was there? Anything to make him run into the street like that?"

"Even the best foster-care arrangements can be terribly frightening to children," Laura said.

"I know, but he ran right into the street."

"Unless you've been through it, you'd never understand."

Laura hadn't meant to say that. He was watching her even more closely with those dark eyes of his then.

"You seem to know a lot about foster care."

"I do."

"Firsthand?"

He'd spoken so gently. Something in his expression had softened, as well. The words sounded somehow intimate, the question growing too personal. The Nick she'd glimpsed in the ambulance, the one who had held her hand tightly and been her lifeline for that long, harrowing ride, was back for a minute, and she found him thoroughly unsettling.

She also didn't want to talk to him about foster care.

Laura merely nodded, then forced her chin up. She wasn't ashamed of anything in her past, and she didn't want this man feeling sorry for her, either.

"Can we get back to this morning?" she asked. Now that she believed Rico was going to be fine, she had questions of her own.

"Sure. What happened next?"

"We talked to the social worker. Or I talked, and the social worker talked. Rico listened and nodded every now and then."

"He still isn't speaking?"

She shook her head, more worried than she cared to explain to this man. "I'm sure he will, once he calms down, once I can get him back to my apartment and we're alone. I'm sure he'll talk to me."

"I hope so."

"What happened next?" Nick asked.

"We were waiting for the final paperwork, so I could take him, when the social worker said there was a policeman downstairs looking for Rico. Rico didn't want to talk with the officer. He was more nervous than before—agitated, even. I tried to calm him down, to explain to him that his mother was still missing and the policeman was going to find her. And then—"

Her voice broke on the last word, and she felt a hand, warm and reassuring, on her shoulder, felt the presence of a man close behind her. She shut her eyes and tried not to analyze the feeling, tried simply to find strength and comfort in the touch of his hand.

"He started to cry," she said, nearly crying herself. "I was trying to reason with Rico. We were in the hallway upstairs, and the policeman was coming up the steps.

"The next thing I knew, Rico just took off in the other direction, and I...I ran after him. The hallways were crowded, but he's so fast. He just darted in and out between people and he got through." Laura had to stop for a minute. "It took me a few seconds longer to get through the hallways, and when I reached the door it was too late."

Laura looked down at the floor through a rush of tears, her voice faltering on the final words. Too late...she didn't ever want to have to say that again. She couldn't let herself be too late to help this child.

Nick sat down on the edge of the bed, facing her, and took her hands in his. Looking straight into her eyes, he said, "It's all right. It's all over now."

She nodded. Her chin came up a fraction of an inch. "I'm sorry."

"Laura, just tell me what happened next."

She closed her eyes, dismayed to find the image all too real. She heard the thud again, felt the terror that had gripped her, heard her own screams fill the air.

"Laura?" he said, low and steady, pulling her back.

"I saw it happen. I saw him. And you," she said quickly. "Flying through the air."

She couldn't hold anything back then. She had no self-control left. In the privacy of the room, with Rico sleeping peacefully beside them and Nick with his warm hands, his beautiful bruised face, she just let loose. A sob first, one that was her undoing, one tear, then another, then this bone-deep trembling that seemed never to end.

Nick hauled her up into his arms, and she didn't even think of resisting. She was never so grateful for the touch of another human being, for the solid weight of a man's body against hers.

She was always the one who did the comforting, who dried the tears and murmured reassurances and hung on tight. She did that for the children.

But this . . . this was something different altogether. Laura realized the difference right away. This was a man, a very unsettling man, holding a woman.

She stopped crying right away and got herself under control, with all sorts of warning signs going off inside her. She couldn't help but notice that he was so much bigger than she was—taller, broader, leaner, stronger. He was solid muscle and heat and power.

He was a man, a privileged one, an educated one, whose life was so different from her own. She wasn't going to lose her head over another man like that. Surely she had too much self-respect. Surely her sense of self-preservation was too strong.

Still, she couldn't quite bring herself to pull away from him totally. Just another minute, she told herself. Another second.

She stood in the quiet, darkened room with her body pressed against his. One of his hands held her face against his neck. The other pulled her close in an iron grip.

Her body was doing treacherous things. Her pulse was thundering, her breathing ragged and shallow, her limbs turned to mush. She felt boneless and breathless in his arms.

"It's all right," he said.

His lips were a fraction of an inch off her right ear, his warm breath fanning it in a way she found incredibly erotic.

"It's all over now."

She imagined those lips against her skin and shivered in anticipation.

Did he feel it, too? Or was she making an absolute fool of herself? Laura pulled away from him just enough to try to figure that out. Was it her imagination? Her own wishful thinking? Or did his arms tense around her for a fraction of a second before letting her go? She couldn't be sure.

But when she brought her head up off his shoulder, when he lifted his head, as well, their lips were about half an inch apart.

She froze. So did he, as if the two of them were held there by some intangible force. She was afraid to breathe, afraid of breaking the spell he'd woven around them.

She looked at those soft, full lips of his. She could have lost him today without ever knowing how it felt to be in his arms or to have his lips pressed against hers.

She wanted his lips on hers. She could just imagine the texture of them, the taste of his mouth, the way it would feel as the sensations shot through her body.

He was going to kiss her; she was certain. He hadn't taken his eyes off her mouth.

Laura closed her eyes, blotting out everything but the image of his face, and tilted her lips up toward his, anticipation rushing like the finest and most intoxicating of champagnes through her veins.

He was going to kiss her.

And then he hesitated.

"Nick," she said, his name sounding like a desperate plea.

Still he hesitated. She imagined that she could feel the struggle going on inside him, her own sense of urgency growing.

A kiss couldn't possibly matter this much to her, yet this one did.

She could feel it. She could taste it. She wanted it so badly that—

He backed away, his eyes refusing to meet hers now, his jaw tensing to the hardness of steel.

Laura's eyes flew open. Her face flamed. The temperature in the room dropped twenty degrees in half as many seconds.

What in the world had happened?

Laura found no reassurances, no clue to what was going through his head. Gone was that lost little boy. Surely she'd been foolish to imagine she'd ever seen anything like that in him.

The other Nick was back, the guarded man with the hint of arrogance who'd so irritated her in the hallway the night before. It was as if a wall had come down between them, as if he'd put on some sort of cold, uncaring mask that he wore at will.

Laura stepped completely away from him, folded her arms in front of her and rubbed her hands against the side of her arms. She was cold, and she decided he must have ice water running through his veins, because he didn't seem to be feeling anything at all.

Laura thought about calling him some vile name. Childish as it was, she would do it—as soon as he tried to deny that something had happened in this room between the two of them. She was certain he would deny it, certain she had nothing to gain by bringing it up, except to further humiliate herself. Surely she didn't need to do that; she'd done such a thorough job of it already.

But she wanted to know—what happened? What went wrong? Like one of those lovesick teenage girls who'd been out on one incredible date with the cutest boy in school, only to never hear from him again, she had to know why he'd backed away like that.

And where did he go? The man who stroked her hair so tenderly. The one who risked his life to save Rico. The one who promised her everything was going to be all right.

She was going to risk the humiliation again and ask. Then the door opened and a man in green hospital scrubs came inside.

Laura couldn't do anything for a minute. She couldn't tear her attention away from Nick, couldn't harness her anger at what he'd just done to her. And then she turned to introduce herself to the doctor. But the doctor addressed Nick first, the look on his face one of surprise.

"I'm Dr. Stephens," he said, extending a hand. "I understand you're a doctor, as well?"

Nick nodded, hesitated, then extended a hand, also. "Dr. Garrett." He looked even warier of this doctor than he had of her only moments before. "Dr. Nicholas Garrett."

"And you're in pediatrics?"

"Psychiatry."

Nick, as cold and remote as she'd ever seen him, watched the doctor. The doctor watched him, then Laura watched as recognition dawned.

"Of course," the doctor said. He withdrew his hand from Nick's, then stared at him with intense curiosity, then something Laura couldn't begin to describe.

Pity? Disdain? Contempt? All those possibilities ran through her mind, though none of them seemed to fit.

Pity? For someone like Nick?

She was thoroughly confused, and it took her a minute to respond as the doctor introduced himself to her. Laura explained that Rico's mother was nowhere to be found and that Rico would hopefully be in Laura's custody soon. The doctor went on to discuss a myriad of possibilities and likelihoods regarding Rico's injuries with her. Frustrated and worried, Laura asked him to get to the bottom line and was relieved to hear that Rico was likely going to be fine.

They were still waiting for some test results to come back, but didn't expect to see any problems. They were going to watch the bump on his head, but unless something unforeseen happened, he could leave the hospital tomorrow.

"Thank you," she said, turning to Nick. "Anything else? I don't even know what to ask."

Nick shook his head, then thanked the doctor curtly.

"Well, I guess now we just wait for this young man to wake up. The nurses have orders to notify me when that happens, but I don't think there'll be any problem."

"Can I stay with him tonight?" Laura asked.

"Of course. We'll see if we can round up a cot for you."

"Thank you, Doctor."

Laura watched him go, then faced Nick. "What was that about?"

Nick gave nothing away.

"That doctor...your name meant something to him, Nick. And then he seemed to recognize you. Why?"

"Ask him," he said, moving away from her. "You'll find out sooner or later anyway. Go out into the hall and ask him. I'm sure he'll be happy to explain it all to you."

"But..."

"I'm not going to talk about this with you. I don't talk about this with anyone. If you want to know, you're going to have to ask him. Or someone. It's certainly no secret. Half the city of Chicago could probably explain it to you."

"But Nick..."

"Ask him."

Laura hesitated for a second, wondering if there was any right way or wrong way to handle this situation, wondering if this was some sort of a test.

She believed him when he said he wouldn't talk about it with her. Obviously whatever this problem was it was too painful for him to discuss. Curiosity got the best of her, and she walked into the hall.

"Dr. Stephens?" she called after him as he made his way down the corridor.

"Yes?" He turned around.

"That man...Dr. Garrett?"

"Yes?"

"You know him from somewhere?"

"We've never actually met." The doctor looked uncomfortable.

"But you know him," Laura insisted.

"Not exactly. I recognized him from the television news and the papers."

"Why?" she asked. "What happened to him?"

"He didn't tell you? And he's working with the boy?"

"No, he's just—" She started to say he was just a friend, but that didn't begin to describe him. "He was at the shelter last night and today. He knocked Rico out of the way of the car. He saved his life."

"Oh, I see."

"See what?" Laura asked, desperate now. "Because I don't see anything. Who is he? Why does his name and his face mean something to you?"

The doctor hesitated. "I don't know if I should be the one telling you this."

"If you don't, I'll go find someone right now who will."

"I don't really know that much about it." He tried to put her off.

"That's all right. You know more than I do."

Still the doctor hesitated.

"I have to know," Laura said.

He paused for a minute, and she thought he was going to refuse to say anything else. Then finally he started to talk.

"There was a boy—a high-school student, I think— who died last summer. And Dr. Garrett was brought up on charges in connection with his death. Negligence, I think, or maybe professional misconduct."

Negligence?

Misconduct?

Nick?

"No," she said.

The doctor threw his hands up in front of him to hold her off. "I really don't know any more than that, and it's been almost a year since it happened."

"I can't believe that," Laura said.

"It was in all the papers. I'm sure it couldn't be that hard to find the information."

Stunned, Laura stood there.

"I'm sorry," the doctor said. "I have to go. I have patients waiting for me."

"Of course," she said, grateful for some time alone to think this through.

She leaned against the wall, then saw a chair nearby and sank into it. She kept picturing Nick, his deep, dark eyes; rich, brown hair; those lips. She saw the bruises and the bandage on his face.

He could have been killed. Rico could have been killed. How many men would put themselves between a speeding car and a little boy they barely knew?

Laura swallowed hard, unable to reconcile the image of the man who'd nearly kissed her with the one the doctor had drawn for her.

She couldn't do it.

With her eyes closed, her head bent, Laura thought about the people with whom she worked, with whom she fought and begged for something her kids needed. As a teacher she ran into selfish people, uncaring people, impatient ones, superficial ones, even negligent ones. She learned to figure out quickly who was a friend and who was a foe.

She thought about Nick, about how much she wanted to believe in him and in her ability to judge people. Could she trust her instincts now? Not just for her sake but for Rico's.

She thought about the bleak look in Nick's eyes, that fleeting impression she'd had of some lost, wounded little boy, then recalled the dangerously handsome man with more than a touch of arrogance.

Which one was real? Which one was the image? Which one was the man?

She had to find out....

Chapter 6

Nick stood there in the near darkness of the hospital room. With his back to the boy lying unconscious in the bed, he stared out into the rain and thought about Laura.

She would know by now, and he couldn't say why that upset him. After all, he had dared her to go ask someone about him. She wanted to know what happened to him, and he certainly wasn't going to explain the whole sordid mess to her.

She had a right to know, he thought. She loved the little boy lying in the hospital bed, and she wanted Nick to help him. Before he did that, she should know what happened with the last kid he'd tried to help.

Sooner or later, she was sure to find out. She might as well find out now, preferably before he kissed her.

Nick snarled at the thought. He wanted very much to kiss her. He should have done it when he first had the chance, because he wasn't likely to get another one.

Strangely enough, he didn't remember the last time he yearned for a simple kiss from a woman. And not just any woman would do. He wanted to kiss Laura Sandoval, teacher beyond compare, defender of little boys and men who'd somehow lost their way.

He wanted some of her optimism, her hope, her determination, to rub off on him. He wanted to try again, to put his life back together, if he could find the courage.

Nick wondered if he'd ever be able to hole up inside his apartment for days at a time again, not doing anything, not wanting anything, not feeling anything.

And he wondered if he'd ever get the chance to kiss Laura, then called himself ten different kinds of a fool. Why did it mean so much to know how she would react to him when she found out all his secrets? Surely she would be like nearly everyone else.

She would see him merely as a curiosity, and she would stare, the same way people turn their heads and slow down when they pass some gruesome car accident on the road.

Either she would hate him for what happened or pity him, and he didn't care to be on the receiving end of either of those emotions.

Nick couldn't let himself care that much about what Laura or anyone else thought of him. By now he should be immune to what people thought. He would go on living just as he had for the past year, at least in professional circles.

If he was in any sort of professional circle.

He paused as he considered that. Was he actually thinking of going back to work? Or considering what he would do with the rest of his life if he never went back to practicing psychiatry?

Did he even care what he did now?

Maybe he did. And Laura was responsible for that change in him.

"Damn," he muttered. He could have happily gone on for a long time without caring about himself or his future, and she'd robbed him of that.

Nick meant to go, but he took one glance back at the little boy lying in the bed. What kind of trouble had Rico gotten himself into?

Even if Nick wanted to make it his business, he doubted Laura would let him near Rico again, now that she knew what had happened to Carter Barnes.

Nick was leaving Rico's room, thinking about escaping back into that black hole otherwise known as his apartment, when the hospital paging system came on.

"Dr. Garrett . . . Dr. Nicholas Garrett . . . please call the hospital operator."

He flinched upon hearing his name broadcast through the hospital, and he could imagine a hundred pairs of eyes following him as he stepped into the hallway. How would he ever get out of this building? He wouldn't be able to leave fast enough.

As he turned and headed for the nurses' station and a phone, he nearly collided with Laura.

She pitched forward. Instinctively his hands shot out to catch her. Nick swore softly as his fingertips curled around the soft flesh of her upper arm.

He looked down at her, half expecting her to tense up on him, to be unable to hold in her displeasure at having him so near now that she knew the truth. But she didn't do anything like that. There was no scorn or pity in her eyes, either. Instead her gaze, steady and direct, met his, her expression unreadable.

"Did you find out what you wanted to know?" he asked as he released her. He'd almost convinced himself she didn't know.

"I found out something that's very hard for me to believe."

Nick wasn't sure how to respond to that. He was stunned. Would she always show him something totally unexpected? He felt something that vaguely resembled hope.

Cautiously, he weighed his options, only then realizing how much he wanted her to believe in him. That need came to him now, staggering in its intensity, frightening him because of the possibilities that had just opened up between them. He cared about her opinion of him, which gave her enormous power over him.

She could hurt him so easily.

Nick wanted her to believe in him.

He stepped back, looked to the left toward the wall and fought the feeling. He'd told her himself that he was nobody's savior. But he wasn't the arrogant, uncaring, even sloppy doctor Carter Barnes's parents had portrayed him as.

He had to warn Laura, to be fair to her and maybe to protect himself. "If you're smart, Laura, you'll forget all about me," he said.

"And if I'm not?"

He swore. She grabbed on to his arm when he turned away from her.

"Did you think of that, Nick? Were you hoping that some bit of gossip would be enough to scare me off? Or did you wonder, just for a minute, what might happen if I wasn't willing to believe it?"

He went so tense he was surprised his veins could take the pressure. He closed his eyes. Hell, yes, he'd thought about that. If that doctor and whatever he knew about Nick's past weren't enough to scare her off, then Nick would have hope. Real, true, honest reason to hope.

Damn her for making him hope like that.

"What did he tell you?" Nick asked. He had to know.

"Does it matter? I don't think it's true, and I don't see why I should listen to gossip when you know exactly what happened and you're standing right in front of me. I'd rather have the truth, Nick, from you, when you're ready to tell me about it, not some half-forgotten memory based on nothing but TV news reports and the papers."

He laughed sarcastically; he couldn't help himself. "I'm sure that man's half-truth was more than enough for most people I know to have tried and convicted me."

"I'm not most people."

She said it softly, almost seductively. He wanted so desperately to believe her, and Nick watched as she came alive again, the she-tiger who'd so fervently defended Rico and his mother to him last night. She was on his side now. How would it feel to have someone like Laura on his side for a change?

"Why don't you tell me about it, Nick?"

"I can't."

"Of course you can."

"I don't talk about it. Not to anyone."

"You?" She couldn't seem to believe that. "A psychiatrist who can't bring himself to talk about his problems to anyone?"

"Ironic, isn't it? My life gets all screwed up, and as a bonus I find out I have no faith in my own profession to help me."

"Nick—"

His name came booming over the paging system again, the request more urgent this time.

Nick was incredibly relieved. He was saved. "I have to answer this. Besides, Rico was stirring when I came out to take this call."

She didn't buy that completely, but she turned toward the boy's room. "Don't you walk out on me again," she challenged.

Nick admired the lady's nerve. Hell, he admired just about everything about her. Wistfully, he walked down the hall and took his call.

He lied to her. Rico wasn't moving at all, and Laura was fighting the urge not to open that door and look out into the hallway to see if Nick had indeed disappeared.

She knew he was thinking about that, knew she couldn't stop him if that's what he wanted to do.

And she still couldn't remember anything about what had happened to him and that boy who died.

The doctor said he was a high-school student, that it happened last summer and that Nick had been charged in connection with the teenager's death.

She thought back to this time last year, saying goodbye to her last class of students, filling out paperwork, catching up on a million things that needed to be done around her apartment, waiting for the new school year to begin.

She thought about A.J. telling her to cut Nick some slack because he'd been through a rough time, thought about the bleakness in Nick's eyes, the way she felt he was being arrogant in wanting her to recognize his name, when actually he was dreading it. Laura shook her head sadly. She had totally misread this man.

Now, what did she hear last summer about a high-school boy being killed? Unfortunately, that wasn't a terribly rare occurrence in the city. And usually the cases that made news were the deaths of the very young—eight, ten, even younger. But Dr. Stephens had said Nick was involved in a high-school boy's death.

She couldn't remember. But she couldn't believe Nick had caused a child's death through his own negligence or some professional misconduct.

Behind her, the door swung open. Laura turned around, and was relieved to see Nick walk in.

"He's not waking up," she said accusingly.

Nick didn't show any interest in arguing that point with her.

"Is something wrong?" she asked.

"I'm not sure."

"Or are you just trying to change the subject away from you and whatever happened last summer?" she taunted.

"Maybe I am, but with good cause this time," he said.

"What is it?"

He shrugged. "I just don't like the sound of this."

"Of what?"

"Whatever is going on with Rico. Laura, when he ran out of the shelter this morning, I was across the street."

"Where we were standing last night?"

He nodded. Some emotion flashed in his eyes. He hadn't forgotten. "I've been over and over it in my mind. I can't be sure, but I think I must have stepped onto the street to cross when Rico ran in front of that car. Otherwise I don't think I would have reached him in time to knock him out of the way."

"Go on."

"I looked both ways before I ever stepped off the curb. There was nothing coming. That car seemed to appear out of nowhere, and it wasn't going that fast. I don't see how the car could have gotten to Rico in time to run him down, because it wasn't there when I stepped off the curb."

Laura was hoping she didn't understand the situation at all. "You mean..."

"I don't think it was an accident. I think someone deliberately tried to run him down."

She swallowed hard, the muscles in her throat not wanting to cooperate. "To kill him, you mean?"

Nick nodded. Laura clamped a hand over her mouth and tried not to say anything for a moment. She might have swayed on her feet, might have made some involuntary sound; she couldn't be sure. But the next thing she knew, Nick had her by the arms. He backed her up until she felt the bed behind her knees.

"Sit down," he commanded.

She sat. He stood there in front of her, looking as strong and as sure of himself as she'd ever seen him, and she sensed that this was the old Nick, the one from before that other boy died, the one in command and in control.

"Oh, Nick," she said, hating what had happened to him, hating what he thought was happening right now with Rico.

"Give it a minute," he said.

His hands rubbed at the tension in her arms, then her shoulders. She sighed, leaned her head back against her shoulder, then, when one of his hands gave her the slightest bit of encouragement, let it fall forward against his chest. He rubbed her shoulders some more, his hands strong, the motion smooth and soothing.

Laura found herself close to tears again as she thought of the implications of what he'd suggested. "He's just a little boy."

"I know."

"Why would anyone want to hurt a little boy?"

"That's what we have to figure out."

We? Did that mean he was going to stay and help her and Rico? Or had he simply used the word without thinking?

She wanted him to stay, and she thought he needed to stay, as well. Last night, one of the kids at the shelter told her Nick hadn't been there in months. He'd simply dropped out of sight. She wondered if he was working at all, if he still had a license to practice.

She hoped that he did and that he could find a way to help Rico, and she hoped she wouldn't make an absolute fool of herself over Nick in the process.

Much as she wanted to stay right there, with her face pressed against his chest, his hands gently working their way across her back and shoulders, she pulled away from him.

"Think about it," he said, stepping back and standing up straighter, bracing himself against her. "Why would someone be after him?"

Laura shook her head, barely able to keep up with all that he was saying and all that was going on between them. Rico. For now she had to concentrate on Rico.

"He lives on the North Side of Chicago, not far from the projects. Kids get killed for no reason all the time."

"In a drive-by, sure, but this didn't feel like the work of a gang. They would have shot him."

"I don't know," Laura said.

"I thought about the gangs first, thought he might have seen some drug deal or some hit, that they might be after him because of what he saw, but it doesn't fit."

"What else could it be?"

"I don't know," Nick said. "He must have seen something that frightened him. That must be the reason he isn't talking. And I'm afraid this may be a lot more complicated than I thought."

"Why?" He was keeping something from her, and she wouldn't let him do that.

"When the hospital operator paged me, I had a phone call from A.J. Someone called her back to the shelter today because a policeman showed up asking questions about Rico. The policeman wanted the clothes Rico was wearing last night and the shoes."

She went cold all over when it came to her. "Because of the bloodstains?"

Nick nodded.

"For evidence? Because they think some sort of crime was committed and he was in the middle of it?"

"Exactly," Nick said. "But there's one little problem. No one could find the clothes. They turned the shelter upside down. Those jeans and the sneakers have disappeared."

Laura was still thinking about crimes and evidence, so she had trouble making herself consider the rest of it. The clothes were gone? She was so surprised she couldn't say anything. This situation just kept getting worse, and like someone who'd fallen into a maze, Laura didn't know what to expect next or where to turn.

Except to Nick. She always found herself turning back to him.

"The shelter is a busy place," she said, looking for excuses, needing to find them. "There were all those kids, coming and going all the time. Someone may have simply stolen them."

"Maybe, but A.J. knows those kids. She checked her list of most likely thieves and came up with nothing."

"Still, anyone could have just walked in off the streets..."

"No, there's someone at the door all night long. He was already on duty when you went back inside last night. You and Rico were in that room, where the clothes were. You spent the night there, didn't you?"

"Yes, but I took a shower this morning before Rico woke up. And I went to the kitchen for some coffee. Someone could have come in then. Or last night, when I was outside with you."

"It's possible," he admitted.

"But you don't believe it."

"I've seen a lot of rotten things happen to kids."

"So have I, Nick."

"And I tend to be a little cynical."

"Tell me something I don't know. What do you think happened to Rico's clothes?"

"There was blood on the clothes. Obviously, someone was hurt. And Rico was there. I think whoever hurt the person whose blood is on Rico's clothes is after Rico now, to make sure Rico doesn't tell anyone what he saw."

That was so hard to believe. "I was just worried about him missing school," Laura said. It was amazing the way things had gotten messed up so quickly.

"I meant to ask you earlier—did anyone come up with any information on his mother yet?"

"No," Laura said, wondering how she'd be able to restrain herself once she saw the woman again. "But she's disappeared before."

"And you said she does drugs?"

Laura nodded.

"Maybe Rico saw something to do with her supplier."

"Maybe."

"It's a place to start," Nick said. "Do you know the name of the detective working the case?"

Laura found her purse and fished a card out of the side pocket. "I talked to two different officers. One of them gave me his card."

"Let me call him and see if he found out anything yet."

She handed him the card. "Nick?"

He looked up at her.

"I'm glad you're here. I'm glad you're going to help us."

He considered that for a minute. Laura held her breath, hoping they were past arguing the point.

"I'm not making any promises," he said.

"I didn't ask for any."

He folded his arms across his chest and leaned back against the door. His chin came up as he watched her, measured her reaction. Clearly he wasn't sure what to make of it.

She took one step closer to him. "I owe you an apology. I think I misjudged you."

She took another step toward him, and he reminded her once again of those little boys at school. They were so good at sending out those signals: don't touch me, don't try to get any closer to me, don't ask anything of me and you won't be disappointed. They were so good at convincing most people how bad they were, that they didn't need anyone or anything. And they all desperately needed someone to see through their act.

Laura could see all those emotions so easily in Nick now.

There was only one problem—he wasn't a little boy. He was a man. Laura knew all about helping lost little boys, but frighteningly little about doing the same thing for a grown man.

A gorgeous, hurt, angry man, she amended. What did a woman do with a man like that, especially when she felt this compelling urge to touch him?

Touch, at its most basic level, was reassurance. She was with him, she understood something of what he was feeling and she cared about him. Those were the kinds of reassurances lost little boys needed most of all.

Laura wondered if she could treat Nick like one of those little boys. She meant to do nothing more than to reassure him, to thank him—a simple gesture with a simple purpose.

But it didn't feel simple or easy anymore. And the urge to touch him only grew stronger.

She wondered if anyone ever touched him anymore, if he deliberately held himself away from everyone because of what had happened to him. She could just imagine Nick locking himself away from everyone.

Some of her kids in the classroom were like Nick— starved for the simplest touch, the smallest bit of encouragement. She gave all of that and more to them. Surely she could do the same for this man who'd done so much to help Rico already.

Knowing that a very big part of what was going on in this room had absolutely nothing to do with Rico or with hopeless cases or lonely people, Laura moved even closer.

Part of this—a big part, she feared—was simply one woman reacting to one man. It hadn't been so long that she didn't recognize the stirring of desire when she felt it—not once she got over the surprise, at least.

"Oh, Nick."

"What did the doctor tell you about me?" he said, every instinct on alert.

"It doesn't matter." She believed that.

"How the hell can you say that?"

Obviously she'd touched a nerve. She tried to reassure him. "Whatever it was, it wasn't true. I'm sure of that."

Laura decided it was now or never. Before she lost her nerve, she brought one of her hands to rest softly against his chest, as a test.

He allowed it to stay there. She smiled, encouraged by the reaction. Maybe he wasn't as far gone as she feared.

"Laura, you need to know that whatever that doctor said, I'm sure at least part of it's true. I screwed up, and a teenager was shot to death because of it."

Her other hand rested tentatively against his jaw. She felt heat coming off him, felt that smooth texture of a freshly shaved patch of skin, felt the way he tensed at her touch. She couldn't decide whether he was surprised by the fact that she was actually touching him or whether he was even more worried than before.

"I don't buy it, Nick," she said, running on sheer instinct now. "Not for a minute."

"It's the truth."

She moved forward, before she succumbed to the warning in his eyes. The hand at his chest she used for balance as she stood on tiptoe.

Laura hadn't been so bold with any man before, but she liked this feeling. She suspected the only reason he let his lips touch hers was that she'd caught him by surprise. Nevertheless, it was working.

"Thank you," she whispered.

"For what?"

"For being here. For trying to help Rico and for helping me."

"Laura." He said it like a warning.

"Admit it, Nick. You are one of the good guys. You told me so yourself, although now I don't think you quite believe it."

"I can't promise you anything," he said.

"But you're going to be here for Rico. You're going to help me help him. I know it. I can tell by the look on your face when you're with him. You care about him. You couldn't make yourself walk away from him now if you tried."

"Laura—"

"Thank you, Nick."

She leaned forward, kissed him softly on the lips, intending to do no more than to apologize for being so harsh with him last night.

That was all she intended—to touch her lips to his. But the instant they connected, she felt something that set her heart racing, her mind reeling. It was electric and powerful and mystical all at the same time. It was a connection involving much more than his lips and hers.

He felt it, too. Her eyelids flashed upward, and she found herself looking into his eyes.

An instant later, his hands closed over hers in a grip that allowed no resistance. He pushed her away, then stared at her as if he couldn't believe what he was seeing.

"Didn't you hear me? I said I screwed up and a teenager died because of that."

At that moment he reminded her of a kid who'd just told her his deepest, darkest secret and was now waiting for the retributions he expected to follow.

"I heard you," she said quietly and calmly.

He looked incredulous. "You can't say that doesn't mean anything to you."

Obviously it meant everything to him. Laura wondered exactly what the last year had been like for him. If he had made a mistake, a fatal one, Laura was sure that he'd been harder on himself than anyone else could have been.

She also had a hunch about something else. "I don't think it was your fault, Nick."

"Oh, for God's sake, you don't even know what happened."

"So tell me."

He shot her a look that said "Go to hell" as clearly as any words could have. "You don't have any idea what you're talking about."

"But I've found out a lot about you in the past twenty-four hours."

"Laura." He sighed heavily, then gazed at the ceiling, at the walls, anywhere but at her. And he still had hold of her arms. "Don't do this to me."

"Do what?"

"Don't butt into my life like this."

That hurt.

"Aw, dammit," he said.

She caught him staring at her then and heat flooded her face.

"Laura..." He was almost begging her. "Don't ask me to make any promises that I can't keep."

"I haven't."

He looked like a man backed against the wall. Painfully, he said, "I haven't worked in almost a year."

She couldn't say that surprised her. "All right. Go on."

"The idea of having that little boy depending on me to help him scares the hell out of me."

She took a minute to think about that. He was scared. She'd never considered that. The mannerism she took for a damning touch of arrogance was actually fear?

She should have seen that. Nick had merely put on some tough-guy act, similar to what Rico had done so many times. How about that? She'd found a man who could admit to being afraid. She liked him even more for that. She knew all about being afraid, although she was sure it was a totally new emotion for Nick.

She smiled at him and wondered if he'd let her kiss him again. She doubted it. And she wasn't sure if she was ready for that anyway. If she felt that adrenaline rush again, that power and excitement skimming through her veins, she wasn't sure what she'd do. Never in her life had she felt so much from a simple kiss.

She settled for nothing more than the smile. "You told me you weren't such a bad guy," she said. "And now I believe it."

Maybe he didn't realize it yet, maybe he wasn't ready to admit it to himself, but he was going to help them.

"Laura," he began again.

She touched her fingertips to his lips to quiet him. "I know. No promises."

He looked thoroughly exasperated. She felt a little thrill of feminine power in knowing that she had managed to unsettle him with a little kiss and a little faith.

"Why don't you go and make that call?" she said. "Rico and I will be right here when you get back."

She had no doubts now. Nick would be back.

Chapter 7

Nick didn't sleep well that night, but it wasn't his usual nightmare that kept him awake. It didn't have anything to do with the shooting of a fifteen-year-old boy.

This time he dreamed of a lovely, dark-eyed woman with hair that never seemed to end and lips that brought the body of a half-dead man roaring painfully back to life.

He cursed her. He shouted at her from within the barren walls of his apartment, the one that now seemed more like a dungeon than a coward's refuge.

He'd been a coward for the past year. It galled him to admit it, but he didn't see anything else he could call it—not honestly, at least.

She made him see that. She'd jolted him out of this safe little hiding place and showed him that he'd grown tired of licking his wounds and doing his damnedest to simply disappear, until all his problems did so, as well.

Laura had done this to him, and he didn't know whether to thank her or to shout obscenities at her, instead.

He was certain of only one thing—he wanted to kiss her again. He wanted to know if it could possibly feel as good as he remembered.

And if it did, he was in even more trouble than he was now.

As he saw it, all he had to do was kiss Laura Sandoval again and prove to himself that it wasn't at all as earth-shattering as he'd dreamed.

If he was smart, he'd talk one of his former colleagues into working with Rico and he'd find a law-enforcement officer he trusted to look after Rico's and Laura's safety.

He'd convinced himself, sometime during the night, that he was being paranoid in thinking someone was after Rico. The police could have easily gotten their wires crossed and sent two people after the same bloodstained clothes.

So Nick was going to take care of those few details, and then he was going to tackle some of his own problems, like how he was going to put his life back together again.

He thought about the mess otherwise known as his life for what seemed like hours, then consulted the clock. Maybe fifteen minutes had passed. His mind remained stubbornly in one place—a hospital room across town with one little boy and one maddeningly attractive woman.

Not long after that, he picked up his coat and walked out the door.

* * *

Between the nurses coming and going to check on Rico, the rumbling and clanging of equipment being wheeled past in the hallway, and the whimpering sounds that Rico made, Laura had little opportunity for sleep.

When the night nurses made their final rounds before going off duty at seven, Laura showered, changed into some fresh clothes a fellow teacher and neighbor had dropped off the night before, then stared at the little boy in the bed.

He was restless, as he had been all night, but still sleeping. The nurses said that if he truly had spent three days and nights on the streets, then it was likely exhaustion and lack of sleep were catching up to him now. It was not, as Laura feared, some kind of complication from his head injury.

She didn't want to leave him yet, but she was itching to get to the library. She wanted to go through some back issues of the paper and find out what she could about Nick and what happened to him and his patient last summer. Laura couldn't believe Nick would have been reckless or careless in his treatment of a child.

Even more curious was the way he never tried to hide the fact that he was involved in something tragic. He worked very hard at pushing her away.

Well, Laura would not be pushed. But she did want to be prepared. It made sense to be prepared, she'd told herself over and over again. She wouldn't be betraying Nick in any way by finding out what she could about the incident. He had invited her to do so when he sent her to talk to the doctor yesterday. So why did it feel like the betrayal of a trust or the invasion of his privacy?

Because she'd kissed him? Because they'd started something and it was still fragile and new? Because she didn't want to do anything to mess things up between them?

All those things and more ran through Laura's head.

She wanted to help Nick, she reminded herself. She wasn't doing this out of some morbid sense of curiosity. Perhaps if she knew more she could help him. And maybe she wouldn't need the newspaper clippings at all—maybe Nick would tell her himself.

Laura debated with herself before finally picking up the phone and calling her friend Connie, who'd brought the clothes the night before, and asking Connie for one more favor.

Rico finally woke up around ten-thirty, and he was clearly happy to see Laura. He puzzled over the bandages on his forehead and the side of his face, and she explained his injuries and what would hopefully be a brief stay in the hospital.

Later, he was a little apprehensive when the doctor came in and examined him. But the boy received a clean bill of health. He could go home soon. They were both relieved.

Rico still wasn't talking, though the two of them managed to communicate through a series of nods and shakes of his head. He didn't exactly remember the car that hit him, but he recalled the noise and the way Nick had grabbed him. Laura was sure he remembered being at Hope House when the policeman had come to talk to him, but he wouldn't tell her why he'd run into the street like that.

She didn't want to press him just yet by asking him to recall anything before he'd arrived at the shelter. Clearly he was still frightened by the whole situation.

So she talked about the social worker, explained that as soon as the paperwork was finalized and the doctor released him Rico could come home with her. He brightened visibly at the news. Laura pulled him into her arms and held him for a moment.

The door to the room opened, and she looked up, hoping to see Nick. Instead she found a uniformed policeman, the one she'd seen at the shelter last night.

Laura didn't like the policeman who came to question Rico. He was in a hurry, and he didn't seem to care that Rico was scared or that he hadn't said a word since showing up at the shelter less than forty-eight hours ago.

And the policeman wouldn't let Laura stay in the room with Rico while they talked, which worried her.

They had nearly escaped the police questioning altogether. In the hallway, the nurses had found her to take a call from Sharon Sawyer at social services. The paperwork was done. She could take Rico home. All Laura had to do was to wait until rounds were over so the doctor could sign the discharge papers. They would be free to go. Now she had to contend with this surly cop, instead.

She thought about calling someone else on the police force—maybe that man Rico's mother had dated off and on for the past year—but she still couldn't remember his name. If she could, maybe he would help. At least he would know Rico. Surely Rico wouldn't be so scared talking to someone he knew.

Laura tried to recall his name. Rico had mentioned him a few times in class. Maybe when Rico started talking again, he would tell her. Maybe this could get him to talk.

Just then the door to Rico's room opened. Laura turned and saw the policeman coming out of the room with Rico in tow, already in the wheelchair the nurses had brought earlier in preparation for Rico's discharge.

The cop looked even more intimidating than before; he wasn't that tall, but he was beefy, with big rounded arms, a rounded chest, a reddish hue to his cheeks and a crew cut. Laura disliked him on sight.

And, if possible, Rico looked even more frightened than before. He was huddled to one side of the chair, his eyes downcast, his expression carefully blank. He had tuned out the world; Laura recognized that pose all too well.

She bent down to put herself at eye level with Rico, but he refused to look up at her.

"Rico?" She placed a hand on his knee and gave him the best smile she could manage under the circumstances.

"We're going to have to take him to the station," the cop said.

"What?" She stood up. "Why?"

"We picked up someone who was reportedly seen near the apartment building last week, and we need to find out if the boy can ID the suspect for us."

"He's not..." She paused for a moment as this surge of panic ran through her. She didn't want this man to take him. "He isn't even talking yet. Did he talk to you?"

"He doesn't have to."

Clearly the man wasn't used to having his actions questioned.

"He can point, can't he? That's all we need."

The man already had his back turned, dismissing her as nothing but an annoyance. Laura was outraged. "What about what Rico needs?" she shouted.

The cop turned around, the flush in his cheeks heightened. She wouldn't want to run into him on a deserted street at night alone.

"Look, lady," the man snapped, then halted momentarily as if to reconsider. "I'm sorry, okay? But I don't have all morning. I can't hold this guy forever without charging him with something, and I don't have time to argue with you about this. I'm just trying to do my job, and I need to take the kid to the precinct house on Third Street to see if he can ID our suspect."

"Then I'm coming with you," she said.

"I don't think that's a good idea."

"Well, I do, and at the moment, I'm his legal guardian." Laura hoped he wouldn't ask for proof, because she didn't have any of the paperwork yet.

"Then you can pick him up at the station when we're done."

The cop just turned and walked away, pushing Rico along with him.

"Hey!" she said.

Rico turned around, eyeing her pleadingly. He was afraid. Couldn't this surly cop see that? The man didn't even glance back. He just kept right on walking.

Laura started to run after him. She didn't care if she looked like some foolish, overprotective parent; she didn't want Rico to be alone with this man.

She was terribly afraid, and she didn't know why. Were other mothers this protective of their children? Or was she being unreasonable now that she was once again wading into the unfamiliar waters of parenthood?

Laura didn't know. She suddenly felt unable to cope with the responsibilities she'd assumed as Rico's foster parent.

Then she saw Nick coming down the hallway.

"Oh, thank God," she said to herself, then reached out to him with two trembling hands. "Nick."

"What's going on?"

He took her hands in his and steadied her. She didn't stop to think about how right that felt and how reassuring.

"I'm so glad you're here. One of the cops came back this morning, and he's taking Rico with him."

"Where?"

"To one of the precinct offices. He said they picked up some guy who was spotted near Rico's apartment last week, and the police want to see if Rico can identify him."

It didn't sound unreasonable at all when she said it, but still—it had felt incredibly wrong to her to let him go.

"And you didn't go with him?" Nick said.

"The policeman wouldn't let me. The man is an absolute ox. I . . . I don't know what to do." Normally she wouldn't have let anyone run over her the way that policeman had, but she was on unfamiliar ground here.

"I don't like the sound of this, Laura."

She was so relieved to hear him say it. "Neither do I."

"I know a few cops. What was his name?"

"Welch, I think. He was one of the cops who came to the shelter the first night."

"What did he look like?"

"A sausage." She smiled at his reaction. "He did. All puffed up and rounded, red in the face, as if he was going to explode any minute."

"I don't think I've had the pleasure of meeting him."

"Believe me, you would remember."

"How long ago did they leave?"

"Ten seconds."

"Then we shouldn't have any trouble catching them in the parking lot."

She smiled again. She was right about Nick. He was going to help her and Rico.

"Let's go," he said. "Which way?"

"This way. I know I'm probably being silly, but Rico was frightened. And there's no reason for a policeman to frighten him."

They made it to the end of the hall, then waited impatiently for the elevators, which finally came and deposited them on the first floor. They were nearly to the front door, when Nick heard his name over the PA system.

Laura looked at him questioningly when he stopped walking.

"I need to get it," he said. "It may be A.J., and she may have found out something about Rico for us."

"Okay. I'll go ahead. I don't want to miss them."

"I'll be right there."

Laura walked out the back doors, where a security guard was directing traffic. He remembered seeing the cop with Rico and pointed her around to the alley to the left. She caught up with the two of them as they reached the police car.

Rico saw her first and gave her a teary smile that did funny things to her heart. But then, she'd fallen hard for this little boy right from the start. There was something about those beautiful brown eyes of his, and his silly grin, that got to her.

"Well, hello, little man," she said. "Miss me?"

He nodded.

The cop, who was unlocking the door of the police car, whirled around, his eyes narrowing on her, the veins in his temple throbbing anxiously.

"What are you doing here, lady?"

"I'm going with you," she said.

He gave her a smirk that said he'd like to see her try it.

The cop opened the door. Laura caught the door with her hand and waited, forcing the man to look at her and to say something rather than letting him close the door.

"I warned you about this," he said, then grabbed her by the arm and pushed her away.

Off-balance, she stumbled and fell to the sidewalk, scraping her knees as she hit.

When she looked up, the cop was walking back to the car. He'd shoved her to the ground, and now he was going to leave her there. He was going to take Rico. Laura jumped up and ran after him, yelling as she ran.

"Hey! Who the hell do you think you are?" She caught him by the sleeve and yanked it to make him turn around.

When he did, she saw only one thing—the gun in his hand—and knew only one emotion—fear, unlike any she'd ever experienced.

"Dr. Garrett," Nick said as he picked up the phone, trying not to think about how many times he'd answered a hospital page like this, how natural it had once been to him, how unsettling it was now.

"Nick, it's A.J. I knew you'd be there."

He decided to let that go unchallenged. He didn't need to ask how she knew, didn't need to hear her say that she knew he wouldn't be able to resist a kid like Rico.

"Where are you, A.J.?" he asked instead. "At the shelter?"

"What if I am?"

"The shelter where you supposedly stopped working two days ago?" He knew her, as well. She'd never stop helping kids in trouble, either.

"Wise guy," she said.

Nick laughed easily. He felt better today. He felt . . . almost normal. Maybe there was hope for him after all.

"What's up?" he asked.

"I'm worried about Rico. It's not like us to misplace something like a pair of bloody jeans, so I called Joe Dailey."

"And?"

"He said he gave the clothes to a cop who came by the shelter late that first night."

"So? The cops just got their wires crossed. One of them forgot what the other did."

"No. According to the cops, no one assigned to work on this case picked up those clothes."

Nick didn't say anything for a minute, but he turned to face the doors, where Laura had disappeared a moment ago to go find Rico and a cop—a rude, overbearing man who had insisted on taking Rico alone with him.

"I don't like the sound of this at all, Nick."

"Neither do I." He wished he hadn't let Laura go by herself. "What was the cop's name?"

"Joe didn't think the man gave his name. And he couldn't remember seeing the man's name anywhere on his uniform."

"What did he look like?" Nick pressed, feeling more uneasy, hating to let any more time pass before he went to find Laura, but needing the information.

"I don't know. I didn't ask."

"Dammit." He backed up and tried again. "When you called the precinct house, who did you talk to?"

"Officer Mitchell."

"He's in charge of the investigation?"

"Yes."

"Did he tell you they picked up a suspect someone saw near the apartment three or four nights ago? That they wanted to see if Rico recognized the guy?"

"No, he didn't say anything about a suspect. He said they're stumped. They don't have any idea what happened there."

Nick didn't need to hear anything else. His instincts were screaming at him. He didn't even take the time to explain things to A.J.; he was afraid he didn't have that much time to waste.

"I have to go, A.J. I'll call you later and explain." He dropped the phone, turned and ran for the door.

Outside, a security guard directed him to the side of the building where the man saw the policeman go with

Rico, then saw Laura follow. She couldn't be that far ahead of him. No way. He couldn't have eaten up more than a minute on that call to A.J.

But then, a minute could mean everything. The world, as anyone knew it, could shift and turn irrevocably in a minute. In a second. In the blink of an eye.

Nick knew that all too well.

He rounded the corner at a dead run. Down in this narrow alley, an otherwise totally empty space, he saw something that should have stopped him cold.

A cop, Laura and a gun.

The gun was between them, in the cop's hands, pointed at Laura's beautiful face.

Nick was thinking clearly enough to realize that he should have turned and run the other way, toward the security guard, who no doubt had a radio and could summon help. But he couldn't bring himself to do that, because that would take too much time.

He would not give the man with the gun those seconds.

If Nick left Laura and Rico alone with this man with the gun it might be too late.

Hell, it might already be too late.

Guns were incredible things—one touch of one little finger against the trigger could blast a hole that might as well be a mile wide.

The thought was insane and obscene and had him nearly paralyzed with fear.

Nick couldn't help but wonder how those kids at the high school had felt that day when Carter Barnes went on a cold-blooded rampage through the hallways, leaving Jason Williams dead on the floor in the foyer near the athletic department's trophy case.

Did they watch the whole thing, as he was watching this, with this sinking feeling in their guts? Knowing it was too late to save poor Jason from the crazy person with the gun?

It couldn't be too late for Laura. Or for Rico. Nick made that promise to himself.

He had to do something. He hadn't done enough for Carter, hadn't been there when the boy snapped, but he was here now for Laura and Rico.

He never had a chance last summer to put himself between the other boy and that other gun, but he had the chance now. And he was going to take it. This time would be different.

Nick ran into the middle of things. Laura looked relieved, and he hoped he could justify her faith in his ability to help somehow. The cop looked murderous. Absolutely murderous. His cheeks and his nose turned beet red, his beefy arms appearing strong and sure of themselves as he leveled the gun at Nick.

At least it wasn't pointed at Laura anymore. Nick had accomplished that much. Now he didn't know what to do.

"You're not taking the boy anywhere," Nick said.

The cop answered by clicking what Nick suspected was the safety off the gun and pointing it at his chest. "I think I'm taking that kid anywhere I want."

Over my dead body.

Nick couldn't help but see the irony in that—this time three days ago, he wouldn't have been that sorry to have this man pump a bullet into his chest, but now it mattered a great deal to him. Now he had something to fight for, to live for.

He was going to help Rico with whatever was bothering him. And he was going to kiss Laura Sandoval at least one more time. If he was very lucky, he was going to do much more than kiss her.

Nick couldn't believe the turn his thoughts were taking with a gun leveled at his chest, but he had two very strong objectives right now—a little boy and a kiss. He couldn't let this madman with a gun win.

"Who the hell are you?" Nick asked, wanting to do nothing more than to keep the man talking enough to give Nick time to think this through. "And why is this little boy so important to you?"

"Who the hell are you?" the man shot back.

Nick could just imagine the reaction he'd get when the man found out he was a psychiatrist. Frankly, he didn't see much comparison between the power of his degree and experience and this man's weapon.

Frantically he searched his mind for something to do. Just then, in the distance, a siren whined. Coming closer? He couldn't be sure. He knew the hospital was behind them. Seems it would be a safe bet the vehicle was headed this way. Now, if only he could remember whether police sirens sounded different from the ambulance sirens.

Who are you? this crazy cop had asked him.

"I'm the man who called the police," Nick said as the sirens grew louder still.

Either there was no difference in the sound of the sirens or the cop wasn't thinking clearly enough to detect it. He looked taken aback.

Of course, he still had the gun, still had it pointed at Nick.

Rico was sitting in the wheelchair beside the car, huddled against Laura. Nick didn't want them that close to the vehicle if the cop should decide to leave with the two of them anytime soon.

"Get away from the car," he said to Laura.

She looked back at the cop, something he couldn't afford to let her do.

"Do it," he repeated.

The cop made a quarter turn to the left, this time pointing the gun at her. "I give the orders around here," he said.

"You stick around much longer and you're going to be surrounded by a half-dozen cops," Nick bluffed, but it was enough to bring the gun back toward him.

"You're lying," the cop said.

"What if I am?" he shot back. "But then . . . what if I'm not? Can you afford to risk it?"

The sirens came closer still. Nick prayed they wouldn't reach the emergency room anytime soon and the cop would head the other way down the alley before that became an issue.

"What are you going to do?" he asked, turning up the pressure.

Laura had pushed Rico to the side and down the walkway about ten steps. It wasn't far enough, but before they could take another step, the gun was back in their faces.

"Lady, does it look like he's in charge here or me?" the cop asked.

Laura said something in Spanish that Nick didn't understand, but the cop seemed to have no trouble translating it. He snarled at her.

"Cops are coming, man," Nick said, determined to keep the man's attention on him. "What are you going to do?"

The man turned from Nick, to Laura and Rico, back to Nick. During one of those shifts, Nick detected some movement to the side. He was sure Laura was up to something.

As the cop turned back that final time, something flew at his face. Dirt, rocks, dust…a cloud of it. From Rico, the kid of the streets.

Nick lost precious seconds fighting off surprise and admiration. The cop was on one knee, coughing and choking. The gun was clutched awkwardly in one of the hands rubbing furiously at his eyes.

"Run," Nick mouthed to Laura, then nodded toward the way they had come.

He lunged for the cop and the gun, but at the last second the gun came up toward him. A sound exploded from it. Nick heard the bullet ricochet off something behind him and to the right. The cop had fired wildly; he was still rubbing at his eyes. He could hit anything or anyone next. There was no way to tell.

Nick was close enough to get one foot on the man. He kicked the cop in the chest, guessed at his odds of getting the gun away from the cop even then. Nick decided he was better off making a run for it. Besides, Laura couldn't move that fast while she was half carrying Rico. He took off after them, scooped Rico up into his arms and ran.

As they struggled to make it to the corner of the building and to what he believed would mean safety to them—at least for the moment—Nick waited for the sound of another bullet at any second.

It never came. Finally they rounded the corner, to see three police cruisers come screaming into the parking lot with lights blazing and sirens blasting.

Laura started to run toward them, but Nick hesitated. He'd never called the cops. Who had? They couldn't have come in response to the shot, because the shot had just been fired.

"Wait a minute," he said.

Laura stopped and faced him.

"This way." He turned to the right and pulled her along behind him. They came to the back entrance of the hospital, the one they'd exited through only moments ago. The security guard was moving cautiously toward them with his radio to his ear.

"There's a crazy man back there with a gun," Nick said, as they kept on running.

They didn't stop until they turned two more corners to the hospital entrance facing the main road. Nick hailed the cab parked at the curb, pushed them inside, then got in himself.

Rico's face was a lifeless gray, the same color as the interior of the cab. Laura's wasn't much better, and the three of them were struggling to catch their breath.

"Michigan Avenue," Nick told the curious driver, who looked ready to kick them out of the cab. "North, and hurry."

The cab sped off. Laura seemed to have a million questions, but he held up a hand to silence her.

She pulled Rico into her arms and onto her lap. He was trembling, his tears just now starting to fall.

Nick didn't even question the urge that had him closing the distance between Laura and him, or this urge he had to protect her and Rico. He settled himself against Laura's side, put his arm around her shoulders and pulled her even closer. She was trembling, as well.

Rico, looking bewildered, put his head on Laura's shoulder. His dark-brown eyes flooded, then tears overflowed again.

"That man . . . he hurt my mama," the boy finally said.

Chapter 8

Nick couldn't believe it. Rico had decided to talk now, when Nick had to ask the kid to keep his mouth shut. Nick didn't want the cabdriver to be any more curious than he already was.

Nick needed time to think. There was some crazy cop with a gun after them. The cop wanted Rico, enough to try to run him down in the street, enough to try to take him by force from the hospital today. Because Rico knew the cop hurt his mother? Or had the boy seen something even more damaging to this cop? If he actually was a cop.

"Nick?" Laura said. "I just remembered something—"

He pressed his lips against hers. He could have found a half-dozen ways to quiet her, but this was the one he chose. He'd been waiting for a chance to do this since yesterday, right after she'd kissed him. He'd thought about it all night long and all day.

So what if his timing was a little off—it was one hell of a kiss.

He meant for it to be simple, brief, almost impersonal, because he had to be able to think relatively clearly afterward, but that was too much to ask after kissing Laura.

Maybe it was the fact that they both could have been killed only moments ago. Danger and adrenaline had a way of heightening all the senses.

Maybe it was because he hadn't kissed a woman in more than a year. Maybe she was just one incredibly beautiful and unique woman.

Maybe he wanted so badly to find someone to believe in him... yes, maybe that was it.

All he knew was ending that kiss was one of the hardest things he'd ever done.

Laura's mouth was incredibly soft and warm and yielding, her lips already parted, the taste of her as intoxicating as a couple of shots of whiskey.

When he managed to pull away, they were both breathing hard. And Rico was right there between them.

Laura looked guiltily at the child, whose eyes were wide and wet with tears.

"Oh, baby," she said, flustered for a change, wiping the little boy's tears away, then concentrating on him alone. "He hurt your mother?"

Rico nodded.

"Not here," Nick warned before she asked any more questions, then nodded toward the cabdriver.

He looked out the window of the cab, still making its way through downtown traffic. There was a train station coming up on the right.

"We've changed our minds," Nick told the driver. "You can let us off at the station."

They rushed out of the cab and into the crowded station. Nick found a bustling corner full of pay phones, and they lost themselves in the crowd milling around them.

"Why didn't we stay at the hospital?" Laura asked. "The police cars were right there."

"Because I was bluffing. I didn't call the police."

"Oh." She paled. "What would you have done when the sirens stopped and the police didn't arrive?"

"I didn't think there were any police coming. I thought it was an ambulance pulling into the emergency room."

"They don't even have the same kinds of sirens, do they?"

"I don't know. I couldn't remember."

She looked dangerously close to fainting then.

"It was the first thing I thought of," he told her, "and I said it."

Laura still looked incredulous. Nick threw his arm around her shoulders and held on tight, just as she held on to Rico. Nick tried not to think about how natural it felt to be holding her like this or how the three of them had become a team through all of this.

"Don't get scared on me now," Nick said to Laura, then ruffled the tight brown curls on Rico's head, until the boy looked up at him with a million doubts showing in his eyes. "We'll come out of this just fine."

"Why do you think the police were there? Do you think someone else called them because of what happened to us?" Laura asked. "Or were they were there for some other reason?"

"I don't think they had time to arrive that quickly if someone called them because of us. Who knows why they were there?"

"But they were right there. All we had to do was tell them what happened."

"Laura, that cop was holding a gun on us. And he had a police car with a police radio. He may also have a lot of friends on the force. He may have accomplices there."

"Oh." She sagged against him as the reality of the situation sank in. "I didn't even think of that. I…I'm having trouble thinking, period."

"We don't have any idea what we're up against," he told her, wishing he could sugarcoat it for her.

"Oh." She waited, considered, then started to talk again. "I was going to tell you in the cab—I remembered something. I'm not sure if it's important or not, but Rico's mother used to date a cop."

"What?" He thought that sounded very important.

She nodded. "Off and on now, for months, and Rico didn't like the man. He made Rico nervous."

"What was his name?"

"I don't know."

Nick looked down at the frightened little boy, his lower lip trembling but mashed against the upper one. Nick had a feeling the boy was done talking for a while. Nick wanted to comfort him, but he wasn't sure Rico would accept that from him. Besides, Laura was right there. She would likely handle this much better than Nick. He decided to leave the comforting of little boys to her.

"See if you can get the name out of him," he told Laura.

"Okay." She already had her arms around Rico. "What are you going to do?"

"I know a lot of cops from the work I used to do. I don't know that I want to call any of them right now. But A.J. has a brother-in-law with the FBI here in Chicago. I've worked with him before, and I'd trust him with my life. And Rico's," he added, then felt his throat tighten. "And yours."

He realized, as he said it, that's exactly what he would be doing—entrusting their lives to Drew Delaney. Laura caught the change in his tone, or maybe she felt the ripple of both surprise and conviction that had gone into those simple words. She was watching him intently now.

He wondered what she saw when she looked at him, what she would have thought of him if she knew how far he'd fallen and how he'd lived merely a few days ago. She had no idea what she and Rico had done to change his life so quickly.

He had a purpose now, a mission—he was going to help Rico, and in the process, he was going to learn to trust himself again. He might even learn to forgive himself and put his life back together.

"Laura, there are a lot of things I need to tell you, when there's time, but this . . . this can't wait. I want you to know that I feel guilty as hell about what happened to that kid last summer, and part of the blame was mine. But I can't accept all of it. A lot of other people failed that boy, as well. I just . . . I hope you can understand that."

And believe it. And accept it. And still find it in your heart to have faith in me.

She smiled at him, despite the chaos surrounding them. "I know that."

Already she'd known that? He was amazed and humbled. What did a man do to inspire such faith from a woman? Certainly he hadn't earned it. He was right—she was one incredibly generous woman, and he felt damned lucky to have met her.

Now, if only he could keep her alive long enough to see what might develop between them.

Nick forced his mind back to the most immediate problem—this crazy cop with a gun. From his spot in the corner, with his back to the wall, he looked through the crowd of people into the station to see if anyone was looking back at them. Seeing no one, sensing no one's attention focused on them, he turned back to Laura. She was standing behind Rico, with her arms around him, one hand ruffling his hair and the other holding him close.

Rico gazed up at Nick with something he read as a cross between trust and terror. The boy knew what was going on. He had recognized that cop. Did he know why the cop was trying to get to him? Or had Rico seen something he hadn't even understood, something dangerous and deadly?

Nick had to know. He had to convince Rico to tell him, and soon, but first they needed someplace safe to hide.

"I'm going to call Drew," he said, then more softly added, "why don't you see if Rico has decided to talk some more?"

Laura nodded and turned to the little boy. Nick fished a quarter out of his pocket and found a phone. Drew came on the line quickly, and Nick told him as succinctly as he could everything that had happened.

"First, where are you?" Drew asked. "Out in public?"

"Yes, we're—"

"Don't tell me," he cut in. "I'm probably being paranoid, but just to be safe, don't tell me. Are you calling from a pay phone? Or someplace that, if the call should be traced, would no longer lead to your location?"

"Yes."

"Good. Where are you going now?"

"If you were me, where would you go?"

"I'd disappear for a few hours while we check this out. Do you still have that apartment you rented last year to get away from those reporters?"

"Yes."

"And there's still no listed phone number, no name on the lease that anyone could connect to you?"

"Nothing." He had sublet a place from a friend who had left the country. Nick had intended to stay only long enough for the media attention to die down. Now that the whole mess was over, he didn't see any reason to move. He didn't care where he lived.

"Good. Go there, and don't come out until I call."

"Okay, you have the number?"

"No, but don't tell me on this line. I'll have Carolyn get the number for me."

From A.J. Drew didn't have to say that. He was being cautious, and he would have his wife do it.

"Now," Drew said, "this man who's after the kid—do you think he's a cop?"

"He had a patrol car this morning."

"And what did he say his name was?"

"He told Laura it was Welch. He didn't give her a first name. We didn't see any name plate on his uniform, and I didn't get the license number on the police cruiser, but there was an ID number painted on the side. There's a six, an eight and a four, in that order, on the end of it.''

"Well, that's something," Drew said. "You go disappear. Don't talk to anyone. Don't answer the phone. You have an answering machine?"

"Yes."

"Don't pick up until you hear my voice on the machine. I'll be in touch as soon as I know something."

"Thanks, Drew."

"Anytime, buddy."

Laura tried not to let her fear show. Rico stood in front of her, stubbornly refusing to say a word. She knew he was frightened, and so very young to be in the middle of a mess like this. But surely he trusted her. Surely he knew that if she and Nick were going to help him, they had to know what was going on, that he had to help them by telling them what he knew.

Laura tried to explain all that to him, but it didn't get her anywhere with the boy. He must have seen something terrible and frightening, and fear alone must be keeping him silent.

Had someone threatened Rico if he talked? The policeman, perhaps, when he wheeled the boy out of the hospital? That had to be the reason for his silence.

Laura hated to think about what he might have seen, but she had to get him to talk.

"Rico," she said, bending down on one knee to put herself at his level. "Where's your mother? You said the policeman hurt your mother. Where is she now?"

He stared straight ahead, as if he couldn't even see Laura. His eyes were this murky, shimmering mass of tears and lights.

"Come on, little man. You can tell me."

Still nothing. No words, no sounds, no gestures, merely mute acceptance of her pleas and her explanations.

Laura hugged him close to her for a minute, then pulled back. "Can you tell me when he hurt her? Before you ran away? Was that why you ran away? Did you really spend three days on the streets? Can you just tell me that?"

But he wouldn't. Or couldn't. He just stood there, stiff and silent.

Laura felt pretty miserable. The situation just seemed to get worse and worse. What could possibly happen next?

Nick walked toward them. She prayed he had some kind of answers, some kind of plan, because she didn't have any idea what to do.

If it hadn't been for him...she didn't want to think of what would have happened. More than likely, Rico wouldn't even be here. The car would have run over him yesterday.

She accepted the fact now that she'd put tremendous faith in this troubled man, and if today was an indication, she'd chosen well. He deserved that faith she bestowed upon him.

As for the rest of it, that totally unexpected kiss in the cab, the way he'd encircled her in his arms and pulled her up against him—that she was going to have to think about for a while, as soon as she had time to think.

"Come on," Nick said. "We're getting out of here."

"Where are we going?" Laura asked.

"My place."

* * *

That was how she came to find herself sharing an apartment with Nick for the evening. They took the train to a busy downtown stop, then walked six blocks to an apartment building near the heart of the city.

No one seemed to follow them. No one seemed to pay any attention to them. And still Laura couldn't bring herself to relax.

Inside the apartment, they locked the doors, closed the blinds, kept the lights off and didn't answer the phone. They let the machine handle two calls from people who declined to leave messages—experiences they both found incredibly unnerving—and two anxious calls from A.J.

Nick wanted to answer those, but he'd promised Drew he wouldn't talk to anyone.

He and Laura rummaged through the cabinets. The contents of the refrigerator didn't even merit a search. They found some not-too-stale crackers, a few canned vegetables, a couple of boxed pasta dishes and a dusty bottle of wine.

"I take it you eat out a lot," she said.

"When I remember to eat."

"It's been that bad?"

Nick simply shrugged and turned back to the cabinets, which had nothing left to offer.

"We'll make do," Laura said. After having a loaded gun in her face, a makeshift meal was of no real consequence.

Nick surprised her by staying in the kitchen and proving to be fairly competent there. They warmed some vegetables, thawed some bread dough from the freezer, left the wine where it was. Rico ate more than either of them, refused once again to tell them anything, then fell asleep in the chair in the corner. Nick carried him to the darkened bedroom.

"The bed is big enough for the two of you to share," he said. "I'll take the couch and listen for the phone."

Reluctantly, Laura followed him into the room, stripped bare of any personal possessions save for the pile of books in front of the overflowing shelves. He had everything—psychiatry, sociology, politics, as well as a wealth of mysteries.

Laura hoped to find some clue to the man, and maybe from the empty room she had. How much of him was empty, as well?

"It's not mine," Nick said, after he caught her staring at the blank spaces on the dresser, the chest of drawers, the nightstand that didn't even boast an alarm clock.

He told her he hadn't worked in a year, so she supposed he had no reason to get out of bed at any certain time. Still, the idea was hard to accept. Nick seemed to be such a purposeful man; she couldn't imagine him sitting idle in this apartment and watching the world go by.

"You don't have to explain yourself to me," she said, all the while hoping that he would.

"I mean, I live here, but it's not really mine. It belongs to a friend—a colleague—who took off for a year to teach in London. I sublet it from him last year when the TV people found my address and started camping out at my doorstep around the clock. And once the reporters finally left me alone, I didn't see any reason to find a new place."

Laura didn't say anything. TV reporters outside his home, cameras chasing him as he went in and out, details of his life and the charges against him available to anyone for the price of a newspaper? She should have thought of those things.

She should be capable of some sort of coherent thought when he was this close, but it was more difficult than she had ever dreamed possible.

After all, he was just a man. She'd known lots of men, worked with them, gone to school with them, even dated a few. And Mitch, her ex-fiancé, was a terribly handsome man.

So this thing between her and Nick had to be something more than that. She was drawn to him, fascinated by him, wary of making one wrong move and having him throw up all his formidable defenses against her, the way he must have fought to keep everyone away from him for so long now.

"Don't do that," he said.

"What?"

"Don't try to analyze me."

She had the nerve to smile. "What's the matter, Dr. Garrett? You don't like being on the other side for a change?"

"Not one damned bit," he said.

"I hated it, too," she admitted, the words just slipping out of her.

"You've been analyzed yourself?"

She nodded.

"Not going to tell me what sent you into counseling, are you?"

"I wasn't in counseling. That was part of the problem. He couldn't stop analyzing me anyway."

"Who, Laura?"

"A man I used to know."

"A man?"

"A professor of mine in college, in Boston. I had an interest in psychiatry at one time."

"And he turned you off psychiatry?"

She nodded. "Most definitely."

"And psychiatrists?"

"I guess I do owe you an apology for that."

"You don't hate most men on sight?"

"I think 'hate' is a fairly strong word here."

"You don't dislike most men on sight?"

"No, I don't. Do you distrust most people on sight these days?"

He winced, but added, "Go ahead. Don't hold back on my account."

"Do you, Nick?"

She had him cornered. The dresser was against his back. He couldn't retreat, if his pride would even consider letting him. His jaw fell into the light from the lamp, looking like something carved from stone. His lids came down, half shielding those wondrous, dark eyes of his.

"Got it in one," he said. "And, lady, you would have made one hell of a psychiatrist."

Nick knew he should get out of there as fast as he could. He should send her to bed—with Rico—and go into the other room.

But he was enjoying talking to her. It had been a long time since anyone had come to this apartment and talked to him. He wasn't ready to let this evening end.

And he was infinitely curious about this other man she had mentioned so casually. It occurred to him now that he knew next to nothing about Laura Sandoval's personal life. He knew some very important things about her—that she was devoted to the children in her classroom; that her devotion did not end at the classroom doors; that she was idealistic, tenacious, beautiful and kind to little boys and cynical, burned-out men.

He was fairly certain she didn't have a husband, but she might well be seeing someone. What if she had a lover waiting for her at home? And how did she feel about this professor in Boston now?

"Why don't we go in the other room?" he suggested, taking what was certain to be a very dangerous step, "so Rico can sleep in peace."

She hesitated for a second, just long enough to worry him.

"All right," she said.

Nick sat down in one corner of the sofa, with his arm across the back, his body turned sideways toward her.

"Tell me about this psychiatrist of yours." Nick couldn't help himself, and he wondered if she saw right through him.

"He's not *my* psychiatrist."

Nick shrugged, thinking it might ease the tension coming over him.

"What do you want to know?" she asked casually.

"Everything. Where did you go to school?"

She confessed the name of an Ivy League school where tuition was more than many people earned in a year.

Nick whistled. "Pricey place."

"For a girl from the projects, you mean?"

"For just about any girl."

She tried to take that at face value. It was true. Her education had come with a sticker price that would have shocked anyone. Still, she'd named one of the poorest, meanest areas in Chicago as her home. He wouldn't be the first man to be surprised and dismayed to hear about her background.

"I had a very nice scholarship," she said at last.

"You must have worked very hard."

He definitely got points for that comment. "I did."

"And your parents?"

She tried saying it without any inflection or any emotion in her voice. It made people a little less uncomfortable that way. "They died when I was in junior high."

"I'm sorry, Laura."

His hand closed over hers for an instant and just as quickly pulled away. She fought the urge to reach out to him.

"It was a long time ago," she said. "And we were very happy together before they died. I had more than a lot of kids do these days."

He nodded. "So you were in foster care."

"Eventually. I had aunts, uncles, cousins. Tons of cousins. And they did what they could at first, but... in the end, that's where I ended up."

Laura took a deep breath and exhaled slowly. Nick was watching and waiting. "It wasn't that bad," she added, "although I have to confess, I made it sound dreadful when I told the scholarship committee my life story. They ate it up. Loved the idea of rescuing this poor little girl who'd suffered so much in her young life. That coupled with the fact that I'm Hispanic and they look so forward to the stats showing they have such a diverse student body had them doing back flips in the interview room."

That won her a deep, husky laugh that sent shivers down her spine. "I wanted out very badly," she confessed.

"And it got you to Boston."

She nodded.

"Where you met the psychiatrist."

So, he was interested after all. That definitely pleased her. "I almost married him. Is that what you wanted to know?"

He tried his Mr. Innocent look on her. She didn't buy it for a second.

"I'm curious," he said. "Tell me about being 'almost married' to this man."

"We were engaged."

"You could be more specific."

"His ancestors came over on the *Mayflower*. His mother was vice president of the DAR. His father was president of a bank. They were horrified at the thought of having grandchildren whose skin wasn't as lily white as theirs."

He turned to the left and swore succinctly before turning back to face her. "I'd say I'm sorry, but I'm not. I'm damned glad you didn't marry the guy."

"So am I. He said all the right things, but underneath, he was just as bad as his parents."

"How did you end up back here?"

"I worked for a year after graduation in this terribly exclusive girls school in Boston, when I was still thinking of marrying Mitch, but it just wasn't what I wanted to do with my degree. They didn't need me the way the kids at Saint Anne's do.

"I kept remembering this teacher I had the first year after my parents died. She was incredible. She was like an anchor for me. Everything around me was so crazy and unreliable and unpredictable, yet there she was. Every day, right there, whenever I needed someone to talk to. She . . . she believed in me. She told me I could do anything I wanted, and eventually, I started to believe it myself.

"Don't get me wrong. Those little rich girls in Boston didn't have perfect lives, but they didn't need someone as desperately as the Saint Anne's kids do. Their whole world is crumbling around them. The drugs, the gangs, the deaths, the poverty—someone has to try to help them deal with those things."

Nick's hand came down off the back of the sofa. His thumb made little circles on the top of her shoulder through her blouse. Laura found it hard to breathe.

"So," he said, "you're a one-woman social-services agency."

"What if I am? You couldn't be that much of a cynic if you worked at Hope House."

"There was a time when I wasn't such a cynic," he corrected.

Laura shook her head. "Are you trying to convince me again how bad you are?"

"Maybe I am bad."

"No, Nick, I'm not buying it. The truly bad people in this world normally try to hide that fact from other people."

"So I'm the exception to the rule."

"Then I guess I am, too, because I'm not buying your act."

He sighed and looked away. She thought he must be fighting against letting some semblance of a smile spread across his darkly handsome face. And then he gave in to it.

"I don't know what to do with you, Laura. Why don't you help me out? Give me some ideas."

It was one of the most tempting invitations she'd ever received, but she managed to let it pass. She'd made real progress with Nick today. And she had hope. She didn't need to be greedy right now. "Just don't push me away, all right?"

He went so still she thought he'd stopped breathing. Then he turned all serious on her. He came to sit beside her, took both her hands in his and stared down into her eyes.

"You are one amazing woman."

He bent his head over her hands. His lips, warm and soft, moved fleetingly over her curled fingers. She felt the touch all the way down to her toes.

"I want you to know something. I don't deserve your trust right now, but it means the world to me."

Laura managed to swallow past the lump in her throat. She blinked back the tears that flooded her eyes, but didn't let them fall. She didn't think he wanted her tears.

She searched for something to say, something that wouldn't seem too threatening to him but would tell him a little of what she was feeling. Before she could do that, Nick dropped her hands and stood up, shattering the intimacy of the moment.

"Look, it's late," he said, backing away from her as quickly as he'd moved forward a moment ago. "We don't know what we'll face tomorrow. Why don't you get some sleep?"

She nodded and tried to hide her disappointment. She'd much rather be with him. "Could you hand me my tote bag over there on the floor beside the couch?"

Laura wasn't watching as closely as she should have when he handed it to her, and she grabbed only one of the handles. The bag was open at the top. It tipped sideways, its contents spilling over the sides and onto the floor, leaving her feeling like a klutz.

"Sorry," she said.

"My fault." He reached down and started putting things back into the bag.

The last item was a series of folded sheets of copying paper. Laura felt her breath catch in her throat. She'd forgotten they were even there, and she made a grab for them. But she was too late.

They came unfolded when Nick picked them up, and she could easily read the headlines from where she stood. He had to see them, too.

"Oh, no." Laura felt like crying again.

Nick's back went ramrod straight. He unfolded the pieces of paper completely and stared at them without saying anything.

They were the newspaper clippings her friend had brought to the hospital that morning at Laura's request. She never found the time to do more than glance at the headlines before the policeman arrived.

"Nick," she began, but had no idea how to explain.

He shook his head and held up a hand to ward her off. "You don't have to explain."

"Yes, I do."

"I told you to go find out about what happened last summer," he said flatly.

And he had. But he needed her to believe in him, as well.

Nick handed her the papers, then turned his back to her, shutting her out completely. "Do you have something to sleep in? I pulled a shirt out of one of my drawers. It's on the dresser in the other room.''

Laura waited. Again she searched for something she could say, and found nothing except ''I'm sorry.''

Her apology only seemed to anger him more. Trust was such a fragile thing, and she'd broken what little had grown between them.

''Go to bed, Laura.''

With a heavy heart, she walked into the other room and found the shirt he'd left for her.

A well-worn basketball jersey that would no doubt swallow her whole.

His shirt.

She didn't think it would be possible to be comfortable in Nick's shirt, in his bed, all night through, all the while knowing he hated her at this minute. She couldn't leave it like this. He had to understand. Laura walked back into the living room.

He wouldn't look at her at all. He stared out the window through a gap in the blinds, and just the way he stood there was heartbreaking to her.

''Nick, you said it yourself. You told me to go find out about it. You said it wasn't a secret.''

She got no response from him.

''I didn't even get a chance to read the clippings yet, for God's sake. You can have them. They're right here. Just take them.''

She waited. He made no move to get them. Laura dropped them on the end table and waited.

''Go to bed, Laura,'' he said, again without turning around.

So she did.

Chapter 9

Nick didn't have a prayer of sleeping that night. Around midnight, he was sitting on the couch, thinking and trying not to look at the newspaper clippings that remained on the table where Laura had dropped them earlier.

Rationally, he knew he couldn't blame her for being curious. He'd never tried to hide anything from her; he simply wasn't willing to explain it to her himself.

Maybe he should have, though. He could think of it as a test—could he talk about it to someone after all this time?

After years of counseling his patients, getting them to voice the things that most bothered them and assuring them that it was the first step to dealing with those problems, could he take his own medicine?

Or would he choke on it?

He had let this thing fester inside him for nearly a year. He was a coward. Maybe he should just come right out and tell Laura Sandoval that and see what she thought of him then.

Trouble was, he now found himself in the unfortunate position of caring what she thought of him. If she didn't want to have anything to do with him once she knew, he wasn't sure how he would handle that.

Maybe he'd barricade himself inside this apartment for another year. Maybe he would see how much deeper he could sink into this hole of his, and when he crawled out next time, there might not be anything left of the man he once was. After all, the bottle of booze in back of the cabinet was growing more attractive with each passing minute.

Yet Nick couldn't take another year of living like this. He couldn't sink much lower and still dig himself out.

He stared down at the folded sheets of plain white paper, thinking of the story of his life, as seen through the eyes of Carter Barnes's parents, printed on the inside of those sheets of paper.

Laura wasn't the kind of person to believe everything she read. He searched for comfort in that belief, searched his heart for the reason she'd hurt him so much by simply finding those newspaper articles.

He wanted her to believe him, to take his word for everything that had happened and accept it, without a doubt. He wanted her to have faith in him.

And she did, he argued with himself. She'd shown tremendous faith in him, certainly more than he had in himself right now.

Nick couldn't help but remind himself that he had goaded her into talking to the pediatrician, all in the hope of scaring Laura away from him before she came to mean something to him.

If only she hadn't kissed him. If she hadn't stood up to him, challenged him, believed in him when there was no logical reason for her to do so. Then it wouldn't hurt to know she was finding out all the sordid details of his life from back issues of the newspapers.

Nick let it go. He had to. It was done; he couldn't change it. Surely the last year had taught him that. He had no reason to get his feelings hurt by this. He should be glad to discover he could still feel, even if the feelings did hurt.

He would tell her he was sorry he had behaved irrationally, then ask her forgiveness.

She'd forgive him. Maybe she would show him how to forgive himself.

Meanwhile, he had a little boy to worry about. Rico's problems should certainly take precedence over his own.

How was he was going to get through to him? Drew needed to know whom he was looking for, and Rico was probably the only person who could help him.

The sooner the man was caught, the sooner Nick could be sure Rico and Laura were safe. He could send them back to Laura's house and turn Rico's care over to another doctor. He'd have to face the fact that he might not see them again once the danger was over.

Shortly after midnight the phone rang, and he heard the voice he was waiting for on the answering machine.

"Hi, it's me."

Drew.

Nick pulled the receiver to his ear, then turned off the machine so it wouldn't broadcast their conversation. "I'm here."

"Any trouble getting to the apartment?"

"No."

"Any trouble since?"

"No. We had a couple of phone calls, though, two from A.J. and two hang-ups."

"Could have been someone selling something."

"Could have been." Nick was careful to avoid using Drew's name, just as Drew wasn't using his. The news must not be good. "What did you find out?"

"Damned near nothing, although I think that tells us a lot."

"It's bad," Nick concluded.

"Yeah. I don't know what's going on. It's something nasty and complicated, and something that has the bureau and the Chicago police very nervous. I haven't been able to get to the information I need from the bureau, not without broadcasting the fact that I know where you and the boy are or that I know what happened to you both today. I don't think you want me to do that."

"No, I don't."

"I did watch the news tonight. They managed to hush up the fact that a man in a cop uniform with a police cruiser tried to kidnap a little boy and a young woman from the hospital at gunpoint, then fired a shot in the alley."

"That's interesting," Nick said.

"Very interesting."

"So what do we do now?"

"Sit tight. Let me dig some more tomorrow. I'm going to have to tell someone what you told me, but don't worry. I'll be careful."

"I know you will. Have any ideas?"

"Seems like it has to be some kind of internal investigation. That always makes everyone nervous and makes it difficult to get information. We must have a very bad cop on our hands."

"Is the guy a cop?"

"The name he gave you was fake. I think I found the car. He must have taken it from the garage. It was in for repairs. No one was supposed to be using it."

"Great," Nick said. "We have a cop who steals cars and tries to take little boys out of hospitals with the help of his service revolver."

"What can I say? It's a crazy world we live in."

Nick would never argue that point with him. "So, you want us to stay here?"

"For now, at least. Tomorrow we can reevaluate. I could always get you into an FBI safe house, if you want."

"No," Nick said. "I don't think it's going to come to that. Do you?"

"I think we can give it another day and see how it shakes out. Do you all have everything you need?"

Nick thought about it. Maybe something for Laura to sleep in, other than one of his shirts. Maybe another psychiatrist for Rico. Maybe another hole for Nick to crawl back into. Somehow he didn't think Drew could supply all that, even if Nick was willing to ask.

"We'll make do," he said. "Did you speak to A.J.? Tell her what was going on? She sounded a little... impatient when she talked to the machine the second time."

"I told her all she needs to know."

Nick smiled. That meant just enough to make her incredibly curious. "I guess our mysterious missing bloody clothing didn't turn up yet."

"Not yet. If our man is a cop, how hard would it be for him to walk into the shelter and pick up those clothes?"

"It would be amazingly easy," Nick said.

"That's what I figured. You three hang tight. I'll be in touch, hopefully first thing in the morning."

Nick hung up the phone, then dropped his head, rolling it around on his neck in a vain effort to ease the tension in those muscles and maybe ease the pain in his head.

Lost in thought, he was unaware of the fact that he was no longer alone until Laura's hands landed on his bare back, midway down and just to the left. He flinched, his head came up and he whirled around.

"You startled me," he said, then fell silent once he caught sight of her in that shirt he'd dug out of a drawer for her to wear.

Obviously he should have taken more care in the choosing. He'd picked an old basketball jersey, and it was much too big. Anything he selected would have been, but he could have easily found something that covered more of her glorious skin than this. It had no sleeves, and big, rounded openings at her neck and her arms. When she moved, the shirt didn't quite move at the same pace as her body. It dipped and swayed, showing him a little more one minute, a little less the next. Curves and mesmerizing hollows, the sensual interplay of muscles in her thighs as she walked, the rise and fall of her breasts as she took in air and slowly let it out—all combined to rob him of the power of speech and to remind him just how long it had been since he was this close to a barely clothed woman.

"I heard the phone a few minutes ago," she said, meeting his eyes for a moment. "I thought... something might have happened."

Nick found his voice with difficulty. "No, nothing. Drew is still digging. He's going to call back in the morning."

She nodded, then drew her bottom lip in, brought her teeth down in the center of it.

Nick had to look away. "How's Rico?"

"Out cold. He hasn't stirred in hours."

If she knew that, it meant she hadn't been asleep herself. It hadn't been his imagination. She'd been in there, her mind racing, just as he'd been awake out here, each thought of her seemingly more treacherous than the last.

The shirt had been giving him fits earlier. She was sleeping in his bed, her soft, warm body encased in what he would bet was nothing but his shirt and a pair of panties. If she moved in just the right way, he'd be able to tell for sure.

They had a madman—a cop, in all probability—chasing them and the frightened little boy in the next room, and he was busy speculating about the various parts of her body.

It was insane. He wasn't some desperate, hormone-crazy teenager. He was a man, one who'd always been able to control himself around a woman.

What was so different about this woman?

Nick couldn't say how he knew, but he would swear she was just waiting for him to make the first move toward her, that she was just as intrigued by him as he was by her, that he could very easily have her in his arms, that shirt of his effortlessly pulled from her body.

He picked up an afghan off the chair in the corner and managed to wrap it around her without letting his hands actually touch her. It was a masterful feat of engineering, and he was proud of himself, until she looked at him questioningly.

He had no choice but to confess. "I thought you might be cold now that the air-conditioning kicked on." It was a lame excuse, but his brain was functioning at maybe twenty-five percent. The sight of her short-circuited the rest.

Laura just smiled. She had him on the ropes, and she knew it.

"I owe you an apology," he said, needing to get this part out of the way. "I had no right to be angry with you for digging into my past."

"It's all right. I wish I hadn't done it. I wish..." She smiled weakly. "Never mind."

But he knew what she wished.

"Laura," he said, thinking that the name was every bit as beautiful as the woman, "is it me, or do you have a thing for lost causes?"

She smiled. He scored some sort of points for his directness. "I wouldn't know," she said. "I've never met a truly lost cause before."

He whistled long and low, then laughed. God, she could make him laugh after the year he'd lived through. Surely that meant something.

"I don't know what to do with you," he said, being as honest as he could possibly be with her. "Whatever you want from me, I just don't have it to give. I don't have anything to give anyone right now. Laura, there's just nothing left inside me. There's next to nothing left of my life.''

"All I want you to do is be honest with me. Can you give me that?''

He considered, then shot with the first thought that came to his head. "I like what you do for that shirt. I like it a lot.''

She flushed from cheek to cheek. Obviously that wasn't the kind of honesty she had expected.

But it was the absolute truth. He was staring now, thinking that the cream-colored fabric did wonders for the color of her skin. She caught him staring. But then, what was a man confronted with such a sight to do? He couldn't look away if he had to.

"You asked for the truth,'' he reminded her.

That was the only defense he had right then. And he was in trouble. This conversation he'd started, intending to put her off, to push her away, seemed to be backfiring on him again.

Honesty? She wanted honesty? That was easy. "Laura, I haven't been with a woman in a long time. I haven't held one in my arms. I haven't kissed one. So these things I'm feeling now, with you . . . I can't say how much of this is real and how much is . . . the timing. And it wouldn't be fair to you for me to . . .''

"To what? To do anything about what you're feeling?'' she asked.

Nick nodded cautiously.

"Let's back up,'' she suggested. "Why don't you stop telling me about what happened in the past? Tell me what you're thinking right now.''

She all but dared him to do it. Nick couldn't resist. "I'm thinking that I want very much to kiss you.''

Laura felt like Dorothy, caught up in the fury of the cyclone that had swept her off her feet and into a whole other world. This was so far from the routine of her everyday life.

They were in danger. They didn't know what was going to happen next or how they'd fare tomorrow. And despite all that, all she wanted to do was kiss him.

Okay, maybe that wasn't all she wanted to do, but it was the only thing she could think about right now.

And he'd said he wanted to kiss her, too?

"I don't see the problem in that," she said, wishing the words hadn't come out so breathlessly. But then, that's what he did to her—left her breathless.

He looked thoroughly exasperated. "I don't think you understand your role in this. I'm the man. I want to kiss you, Laura, and you're supposed to stop me."

She smiled and wished he'd come closer. "I am? I guess I'm not very good at this sort of thing. I don't know my lines."

"It doesn't have anything to do with knowing your lines. It's called self-preservation. Didn't anyone ever teach you about that?"

She took that first step for him. "I think I flunked self-preservation."

"Lady, you damned well should repeat the course. I'm surprised that fancy Boston college of yours let you off so easily."

The look he threw her way then sent a blush all the way down to her toes. She felt next to naked in this shirt of his, especially now that he was standing in front of her. He was nearly a foot taller than she was, and she thought he must be able to see all the way down to her belly button the way the shirt's scooped-out neckline fell across her breasts.

Laura wasn't the least bit ashamed or embarrassed. She was somewhat surprised at her wanton behavior where he was concerned. But the flush to her skin was from the heat—pure, physical heat. It must be ninety degrees in this room, and it was all his fault.

And he thought she was going to put a stop to this? She smiled again, dangerously.

"Don't do that," he warned.

She ignored him yet again, thinking he was much like the sleek, dangerous-looking, half-grown puppy who lived two doors down from her—all bark and no bite. And she upped the stakes by letting the afghan drop to the floor.

Nick's jaw clenched. The muscles in his arms tensed. And suddenly, he looked as if he were carved in stone.

"What are you so afraid of?" she asked.

He flinched. She wondered if she could really gain some ground by going ahead and calling him a coward. "Nick?"

"I'm afraid you're going to get hurt. That I'm the one who's going to hurt you."

"You're not the kind of man who makes a habit of hurting women, are you?"

"No, but I've done a lot of things in the past year that I never did before. I don't want to add hurting a woman like you to that list."

Laura figured it was now or never. She was going to lose her nerve if she didn't make a move soon. She took another step toward him, then put her hand in that thick, rich, tangle of his hair. It was soft and full and silky, just as she knew it would be.

The pressure of her hand on his head forced his face down toward hers. Already she thought she could feel that little sting of awareness that would shoot through her at the touch of his lips to hers. It was something elemental and all-powerful. Something bewildering and magical that had the ability to melt her from the inside out.

"It's a kiss, Nick," she said, lying about that altogether. "Just one kiss."

She saw the battle going on within him, saw the heat flash in his eyes, telling her he was just as aware of her as she was of him, that he, too, already knew exactly how this would feel.

His eyelids came down, shielding his eyes. His lips parted ever so slightly, giving her hope.

"It's going to be a hell of a lot more than one kiss," he said, "and you know it."

Then he gave in. With a curse and a hold on her that would tolerate no resistance, he pulled her to him. His lips covered hers finally. His body was rock solid against hers. He had just put his hands on her, and already she could feel the hard, throbbing pressure of his body against hers, the clear sign of his arousal that he could not hide.

That burst of awareness came on like a firecracker, popping and flashing around them. Everything else in the world just fell away, until there was nothing but him and her, alone in the darkness.

He kissed her greedily, hungrily, forcefully, as if he simply couldn't get enough of her, as if she were going to be snatched away from him at any moment.

Laura feared the same thing herself—that at any moment he could push her away—and she didn't want that to happen. She wanted to hang on to him, to kiss him, to hold him, to blast through this barrier he'd erected around him and find the man inside.

No pretense. No warnings. No prevarications.

She wanted Nick in every way possible.

She felt her breasts, loose within the dubious confines of his shirt, crushed against a broad, masculine chest. She felt his arms locked around her, then felt the pressure ease as his hands drifted lower until he was palming her hips in either hand and lifting her off the floor, settling her more intimately against him.

She allowed herself just a second to be unsure, because it had been so long for her, as well, and because this kind of overwhelming, undeniable sexual pull was so new to her. Then she pushed the thought away.

After all, this was Nick, and he had more than enough doubts for the two of them. She couldn't afford to have any.

His mouth still held hers a willing captive, and she felt a growing, throbbing heat low in her belly. His hands were still pressed against her hips, his body pulsing in time with hers. It would be so easy, she thought. His hands slipped beneath the cotton panties she wore and his palms pressed against heated flesh. His body thrust gently against hers now, something that, if possible, made her pulse pound even harder and faster than before.

She still couldn't get close enough to him, couldn't get enough of a hold on him to make her think he wasn't going to slip away at any minute.

The kiss moved to a fever pitch then, until he felt like a lifeline to her. She was alive and deliriously happy at this moment to be a part of him. But she wanted more. She wanted much, much more, wanted all that he had to give.

And then there was nothing. Everything simply dissolved into nothing.

No hands on her hips holding her close. No broad chest against hers. No heart beating in time to hers. No mouth plundering hers.

He was gone, even if he was standing right in front of her.

Breathing hard, Laura put her fingertips to her trembling lips, to the spot where his lips had rested only a second ago, then pulled them away just as quickly as he caught her in the gesture.

He turned sideways, putting his body at a right angle to hers, and he was standing about two feet away. He was looking up at nothing, his hands crossed in front of his chest, his stance one of a man she suspected was wishing he were anywhere in the world right now except where he was, with her.

He'd done it. He'd thrown up that barrier. She'd gotten a little too close to him, and now he was going to try to regain ground she wasn't willing to give back.

Laura watched as his mouth opened, as he started to say something she couldn't bear to hear. She cut him off before he could. "Don't you dare tell me you're sorry."

"All right. I won't."

Which was every bit as bad, she realized, because he still felt sorry. He was sorry he'd ever touched her.

"Damn you," she said.

"Yes, that's exactly what you should do, Laura."

She glared at him through tear-filled eyes as she tried to bring her breathing under control.

"You know, if you're so determined to convince me what a terrible person you are, why don't you just tell me what happened last summer? Tell me why I should hate you, Nick. Make it easy for me, and then you won't have to be constantly pushing me away from you."

He glared at her.

"Go ahead," she challenged. "It would save us both a lot of trouble in the end."

He was a formidable man when he was angry—big, broad shouldered, flashing dark eyes, the anger simmering so close to the surface she expected a flash of something resembling lightning.

She could just imagine Nick the fighter, working as hard to save a kid as he was working right now to push her away from him. He would have been a fierce opponent, a true champion to the kids with whom he worked.

She could see it all so clearly in him now, buried inside him. What had done that to him? What had changed him and taken all the fight out of him? It had robbed him of something absolutely vital to anyone who worked with troubled kids. It had taken his belief that he could still make a difference to those kids.

Without that hope and that faith, he'd never be able to do the job. There were too many hurt, neglected, damaged kids, and once a teacher or a counselor or a psychiatrist lost his faith that the kids could change, that they could still be helped, there was no point in going on.

That's where Nick was—he couldn't see why he should go on.

And it was up to Laura to show him.

That's why she was pushing him right now. Even when he was mad as hell like this, she wasn't afraid.

There was no more room for doubts. If only she could make him see that.

"Go ahead. I dare you. Tell me something that will make me hate you."

"Why are you doing this?" he asked.

"You're the psychiatrist, Nick. Haven't you figured it out yet?"

"No."

"I've already decided to trust you, to have faith in you."

"That's totally illogical," he said.

"Maybe so, but it's true."

He considered that for a minute. "Lady, you need a keeper."

"Can I take that as an application for the job?"

That won her a smile and gave her enough guts to continue. "Nick, didn't anyone believe in you this whole time? Didn't anyone trust you? Did you go through this whole mess alone?"

He smiled sarcastically. "You would have made one hell of a psychiatrist."

"And you're stalling."

"Yes, I am."

"You have been all alone, haven't you?"

"Not totally. There was someone a lot like you, whom I couldn't seem to push away, no matter how hard I tried."

"And he..." Laura felt so foolish all of a sudden when she realized she didn't know if he was talking about a man. He might well be talking about a woman.

She'd thrown herself at this man twice now, and had never considered the fact that there might well be a woman in his life, or at least a woman in his past.

"And...he?"

"She," he said softly.

Chapter 10

Laura turned away as quickly as possible and closed her eyes. The only thing she was capable of saying was "Oh." Let him make what he would of that. She was incapable of caring at this moment.

She felt like an absolute fool. Why would she ever think a man like him wouldn't already have a woman?

Then it was Nick's turn to crowd her. He walked around the room until he came face-to-face with her, then caught her chin in his hand, softly stroking it with his thumb, sending her senses reeling with nothing but that slight, sweet touch.

"Don't do this," he said.

"Do what?"

"Don't read something into this that simply isn't there."

Into what? she thought desperately. Into the way he'd kissed her? The way she'd responded to him? Or into his confession that there was another woman in his life who also hadn't taken no for an answer when he'd tried to shut himself off from her? She wasn't supposed to read anything into what? Laura didn't know. There was no way she was going to ask.

"So," she mumbled, then tried to smile, "you haven't been alone through this whole mess after all. I'm glad for you, Nick. No one should be totally alone in this world."

"It's A.J.," he said.

He was watching her, and much too closely for her own comfort.

"She's married," Laura announced, as if he weren't aware of that. She felt even more foolish than before.

"She's a good friend, Laura."

"Oh?" And just what did that mean to him? Would he say that she and he were "good friends" someday?

Nick stared down at her. Laura held her breath and tried not to flinch.

Nick took her hand in his then, a gesture that surprised her.

"Come and sit with me," he said, pulling her over to the sofa. "This is going to take some time to explain."

She followed him and sat in the corner, only then remembering she was wearing nothing but his jersey and a pair of panties. The jersey covered no more than half her thighs now that she was sitting down, and she wished she'd kept her bra on when she'd gone to bed.

Nick bent to pick up the afghan, then wrapped it around her shoulders once more. She didn't know what to make of the look he gave her as he covered her with it.

Laura curled her legs up under her and turned sideways to face him, trying not to think of the things they'd done together not five minutes ago in this room. It was a battle she was sure to lose, especially now that she knew about him and A.J., or at least now that she knew there was something between him and A.J.

He sat down beside her. "Comfortable?"

No, not in the least, though she wasn't about to admit that to him. Laura nodded and looked at the floor.

"Okay." He put his arm along the back of the sofa, where it was very nearly touching her shoulder. She could almost feel the not-quite-there touch.

"I don't know where to start," Nick said. "I haven't talked to anyone about this."

Laura waited, not saying anything, giving him the time he needed.

"I used to work at Hope House," he said finally, "and a few other shelters throughout the city at one time or another. I met A.J. at one of those, eight or nine years ago, and she's probably the reason I kept working with runaways. She was a runaway herself at one time."

"A.J.?" That did surprise her. "She seems . . . so sure of herself, so in control."

"She is—now. In fact, I'm surprised you didn't recognize her, either. Don't you ever watch the television news?"

"Not on a regular basis. It depresses me." Even more depressing was the idea that A.J. was someone famous.

"Remember about eighteen months ago, the stories about a little girl named Annie McKay?"

"The girl who was kidnapped? The one who finally found her family after . . . what was it?"

"Ten and a half years," Nick said. "A.J. is Annie McKay."

"Oh, my God." Laura couldn't believe it. The whole city had been amazed by the story of the little girl who'd been kidnapped at thirteen and presumed dead for all those years. And then Laura remembered something else. "You're the one who put it together, aren't you? You're the psychiatrist who made the connection between A.J. and that poor little girl."

"Yes."

"I remember you now." She'd seen his face on TV as well when someone had interviewed him about repressed memories. A.J. had blocked out everything of her previous life. Laura could see Nick so clearly now, explaining the way the mind works at times, explaining that it was impossible to run away from your past entirely. "You looked so different then."

"I was different then."

Laura remembered. He'd been happy, triumphant almost. "She must love you very much."

His expression told her he didn't understand at all.

"For giving her family back to her," she explained.

"A.J. is very much in love with her husband, who had as much or more to do with giving her back her family as I did."

"Oh." Laura wondered if she was seeing traces of bitterness in him, then decided it was more a sadness, a resignation to the facts as they existed today. So, A.J. didn't love him, not the way she loved her husband. But that didn't mean Nick had fallen out of love with A.J.

"Anyway," Nick said, "when I met A.J., she was just another lost kid living on the streets, and I was still in school, still working on my degree, trying to figure out what sort of practice I wanted to have when I finally finished my training.

"I saw A.J. overcome so many obstacles. She's an amazing woman. She made me believe that anything was possible. I thought, with the proper help any kid could turn his life around, just as A.J. had. I was hooked on psychiatry and on working with troubled kids."

"And then something happened?"

He nodded.

"Tell me, Nick."

"It's not a very pretty story."

"I didn't expect it would be. Tell me what happened. Tell me what changed inside you."

He shrugged uneasily. "Before, I never doubted that I'd done my best for a child. I never questioned my own judgment this way. I never saw the other side of the power to help, which was the incredible power to hurt someone when I failed to do my job the way I should have. I never felt so responsible for the death of a child."

"You said the responsibility wasn't all yours."

"It wasn't. I can see that now. I can reason to the point where I'm certain it wasn't all my fault, but...knowing it was only partly my fault doesn't seem to help. Someone's son is dead, and I think I could have stopped it. I think I misread the situation, and I didn't do enough to stop it."

He hesitated again, shoved his hands in his pockets, leaned against the back of the sofa and stared at the ceiling. "I don't even know where to start, Laura. I haven't told anyone about this mess in months—not since the preliminary hearing."

"Hearing?" Laura didn't remember that.

"Well, we never actually made it to court. I wish now that we had. The Barneses had months to tell any reporter who'd listen how incompetent I was, and then the whole thing was over. They dropped the suit, acted as if it was simply too painful for them to go on, told everyone that nothing would bring back their dead son, so they magnanimously decided to let me off the hook."

Laura was lost. "From the beginning, Nick. Start from there."

He sighed, then settled into the sofa beside her. "I did a lot of different things. I volunteered at some of the shelters throughout the city. I did some work with the DA's office helping them question children who were witnesses in sensitive cases or children who were victims of crimes. I testified in court as an expert witness at times.

"But I had a practice downtown where I took care of the rich kids and earned a good living."

He continued to stare at the ceiling, his fingers drumming against the top of a cushion. She wondered if he was even aware of the nervous gesture.

Nick cleared his throat and continued. "Two years ago, a fifteen-year-old named Carter Barnes III came to see me. It's been all over the newspapers, so it's not like I'm breaking some doctor-patient confidentiality rule by telling you."

"Okay," she said.

"Carter had some real problems, and he needed help. More than he could get from me in a counseling session once a week. Carter frightened me, and I talked his parents into putting him into a residential treatment center here in the city.

"That was fine for two months. Carter was showing some signs of improvement. I thought he was going to be okay. And then someone resigned from the school board in the suburb where Carter's parents lived, and Carter's mother decided she wanted to run for that seat.

"Apparently, she came from a longtime politically active family, and she saw this as her first step into politics. All of a sudden, the idea of having a really mixed-up kid in some residential treatment facility seemed like an incredible liability to her.

"After all, she would be asking people to let her help run their children's public-school system, while she had a truly troubled child of her own who went to some fancy private school in the suburbs when he wasn't in a psychiatric hospital."

"Oh, no," Laura said, the case finally starting to sound familiar to her.

"Yes. I knew it would come back to you. The Barneses signed Carter out of the hospital one day. I fought them on it, Laura. Honest to God, I fought them."

"I believe you."

"Thank you."

He breathed a little easier then, and he stared at her, his eyes so dark, his gaze so intense. She wondered what he saw when he looked at her. She was just a woman who was willing to listen to him, who was willing to give him the benefit of the doubt. Sometimes he acted as if she'd given him the moon instead of something as simple and as basic as a little trust.

She didn't want to think about how difficult the past year had been for him.

"So," he continued, "they took Carter home with them and put him into summer session at that fancy school of his, so he could make up some of the classes he flunked in the spring. They put him back into his old life as if nothing had happened, and I knew it was a mistake.

"I tell myself I fought them as hard as I could without totally alienating them. I was afraid that if I made too big of a stink about them taking Carter home, the Barneses would pull me off Carter's case. And I wouldn't have minded that, if I could've been sure the Barneses would hire another psychiatrist and get Carter the help he needed. But I didn't know if they'd do that. I was afraid they'd end his treatment altogether.

"That's what I'd like to believe, Laura. I've tried to convince myself that was how it happened."

"But you don't believe it?"

"I don't know anymore. It's all such a jumble. I was working on dozens of cases at the time. There were tons of kids at the shelter who I thought were in much more desperate shape than Carter.

"Maybe I didn't push his parents as hard as I should have when they took him out of the hospital. Maybe I didn't work hard enough to convey to them how serious the situation was—I don't know anymore. I've spent most of the past year trying to figure it out, and I just can't."

Laura picked her words carefully. "Did you ever think that you were being too hard on yourself?"

"A boy is dead," he said, raw anguish in his words. "An innocent boy. How hard am I supposed to be on myself?"

Now Laura remembered what had happened. One day, not long after he was released from the hospital, Carter Barnes went to that expensive school of his with a revolver and started shooting. Before anyone could stop him, another boy, who just happened to get in Carter's way that day, was dead.

The way the Barneses told the story, they had had no idea how ill their son was. They had trusted Nick to tell them, and he'd let them down. The Barneses told their story to anyone who would listen, all the while making Nick out to be the villain.

"I do recall it now," Laura told him. "What happened to Carter?"

"He took a plea bargain. He's in another hospital. He'll probably be there for a long time, and that's where he needs to be. But it shouldn't have taken the death of another boy to get Carter into treatment."

"What happened to you?" Laura asked softly, already knowing the basic answer.

Nick leaned forward, put his elbows on his knees, his head into his folded hands, and sighed. Finally, he looked up and told her, "I fell apart. Do you know why?"

She shook her head.

"I'd lost patients before, and it's hell. But with them, I knew I'd done all I could to help them. I know psychiatrists can't save everyone. I could accept that if I worked at it hard enough.

"But I'd never watched an innocent child shot down. I didn't understand the risks at all. I never thought, in doing this job, that I'd make the kind of mistake that would cost an innocent child his life. And when I realized that, I couldn't do the job anymore.

The risks were just too high. Unfortunately, by then the job was my whole life.''

"And it was gone," Laura said.

He nodded, a wry smile on his face. "But I can't do it anymore."

"So you're going to lock yourself away in here until . . . what?"

He looked to the left where she sat. Over his folded hands, his eyes came up. Something flickered through them, some emotion she couldn't name.

"Until you," he said softly.

Inside her all her logic, all her caution, all her fears just melted away. She felt weak, a little dizzy, and this whole conversation became more important than ever before. He was more important to her than ever before.

These things she felt for him—the compassion, the concern, the admiration—had been nothing more than a front, a disguise, for the real emotion underneath.

Laura Sandoval was falling for this brokenhearted man. And it was up to her to mend his heart, because only then could she make his heart her own.

Fear came rushing back full force. This was much more than she'd bargained for. He meant more to her than her ex-fiancé ever had.

The implications were staggering. She leaned back into the cushions of the sofa and dared to look at him again.

"Surely you knew that already," he said. "You and that little boy in there have changed me already. You've made it impossible for me to waste away inside these walls anymore. I don't know if I can pick up the pieces of my life and go back to the work I used to do, but I can't just sit here hiding from the world any longer.''

He waited. She didn't say anything. Laura gazed at the hands clutched together in her lap and saw that they were trembling. Her heart, if it had been hooked up to a cardiac monitor, would have been dancing off the charts. And when she glanced around too quickly, she found that the room wasn't quite steady.

His gaze was, and it seemed to bore right through her.

''You're going to have to help me here,'' he said.

She had to fight to clear her throat enough to be able to ask, ''How?''

''How do you thank someone for saving your life?''

''I don't...''

''Because that's what you did.''

He was more certain of himself than she'd ever seen him.

''I couldn't go on living the way I have these past months. I sank so low I didn't think anyone could have pulled me out. I didn't want to come out, Laura.''

''We...we just needed help, and you were there.''

''There's a lot more to it than that. You wouldn't take no for an answer.''

''It's a bad habit of mine.'' She found the strength to smile then.

''No, it's not,'' he said. ''It's not a bad habit at all.''

Laura thought that was one of the nicest things a man had ever said to her.

Nick took a strand of her hair between his fingertips and rubbed it around. She stiffened in surprise, and he pulled his hand away.

"So, tell me something. Do you think you could still stand to have me touch you? Now that you've heard the whole sordid story?"

"It wasn't that," she insisted. She was thinking of his very good friend, A.J., the other woman who refused to give up on him.

"Liar," he said.

Laura decided her best bet was to go back to the subject at hand because she wasn't ready to deal with this other woman in his life right now. Everything inside her was still too new, too raw in its intensity. "I don't think it was your fault, Nick. Do you?"

He shook his head noncommittally. "The dead boy's parents do."

"I'm sure they got the Barneses' version of the facts, not yours."

"Hell, everybody in Chicago got the Barneses' version of the facts. Nobody heard mine. Nobody cared. After the Barneses stood with a camera and a microphone in their faces for two months straight, never once closing their mouths, nobody cared what I had to say."

Laura observed him. She didn't see a neglectful man or a reckless one, and certainly not an unfeeling one.

"I care," she said. Even if he was in love with another woman.

"Laura..." Once again he stroked her hair, teasing the ends, then taking it in his hands and holding on. "I don't deserve that. I don't deserve you."

"You don't deserve what happened to you last year."

"I wish to God I believed that."

"I think you do, deep down. If not now, you will someday soon."

"I hope so." He still held on to her hair, smoothing it down now. "If you and Rico hadn't come along when you did, I don't know what I would have done with myself. I don't know what I'm going to do with you right now."

She laid her cheek against the palm of his hand and had to remind herself to breathe. She thought of all the things that had happened today, of the incredibly small amount of time she'd known this man, of all that could happen in the next day or the one after it.

With the feel of his hand on her cheek, she thought of all the moments they had between now and the time the sun came up. She didn't want to waste one. She didn't want Nick to retreat inside that shell of his in the broad light of day and dismiss all that had happened on this night.

He would likely start rebuilding that wall of his in the morning. She knew how to tear it down before he ever got started. She wanted to spend the night with him, drawing him closer to her, pulling him back toward life until he couldn't bear to withdraw from it or from her.

She couldn't help herself anymore. She was a fighter, and she was going to battle for him.

Somehow she found her voice and asked, "What do you want to do?"

For a moment, he looked as if he couldn't quite believe what he was hearing.

"If you could do anything you wanted," she suggested, "right now, what would it be?"

"I want to forget everything that's happened, for just a little while."

His palm stayed against the side of her face, but his thumb was wandering across her lips, the touch almost like a kiss.

Almost, but not close enough.

Laura wanted more, much more. "What else?" she prompted.

"I don't want to do anything but feel. I want my arms around you. I want your lips and your hands and your mouth on me, and I want to be a part of you. I want to be so far inside you that I can't figure out where my body stops and yours begins."

Her face flamed at the graphic images that came so quickly into her mind.

"What about you, Laura. What do you want?"

She closed her eyes, yet still saw his face, still pictured his body joined with hers. "I want the same thing. I want to forget about everything and everyone but you."

"Just for tonight." That was all he was offering her. "You have to understand that part of it. Because I don't have anything else to offer you right now."

"Just for tonight," she agreed.

Everything became so awkward then. She waited, thinking he would kiss her, that the kiss would push every other thought out of her head. But he didn't kiss her. He just stared at her, as if he had as many doubts as she did about taking this next step.

And that left her too much time for her own doubts to take root. Maybe he didn't really want to be with her. Maybe he wanted A.J. Maybe he wasn't that attracted to Laura. Maybe she would regret this come morning.

"I need..." she stammered, then tried again. "I want to check on Rico, to make sure he's settled, so we won't...be disturbed."

She bolted from the sofa and walked into the bedroom, only to have Nick follow her and stop in the doorway. The room was dark, the boy snoring softly under the covers. "I guess we don't have to worry about him."

She turned, not knowing what else to do with herself, not knowing how to begin to seduce a man.

"Look in the top drawer in the nightstand," Nick said.

She did, finding a small box of condoms.

"Something left behind by the man I sublet the place from," Nick explained.

She was rattled enough that she hadn't thought that far ahead, but she was glad he had. She managed to get one out of the box, then walk across the room and give it to him.

He took hold of her hand and wouldn't let go, though there was nothing threatening about his grasp. "We don't have to do this. We don't have to do anything, unless you want to."

"I do. I'm just...a little nervous."

He squeezed her hand. "I don't make a habit of this."

"Neither do I."

"I know that, Laura. Everything is going to be fine, for tonight at least. Trust me on that. After that...who's to say. Now, come into the other room and tell me what's really bothering you."

They walked into the living room and closed the bedroom door behind them. Nick tugged on her hand, and she followed him into the kitchen, where he opened the bottle of wine they'd discovered earlier in their search of the cabinets. She said nothing as he poured a generous serving into one glass and handed it to her, then poured another for himself.

"Well?" he said. "It's harder when you take the time to think about it, isn't it? It would have been much easier if we'd finished what we started on the sofa. But I want you to think about it, Laura. I want you to be sure, because I'm certain right now that you have your share of doubts."

She thought of a number of men who would never have shown a woman this kind of consideration, and she was happy that he had.

Still, now that he'd given them this time, she couldn't help but wonder what she was going to do if he said he was in love with another woman.

Would she still go through with this? Would she be able to make him forget about A.J.? After all, he'd said himself that A.J. was very much in love with her husband; she was expecting his child. What could be left between Nick and A.J.?

What could there be between Nick and Laura?

Laura took a sip of the wine, then another. This wasn't going to get any easier. "About you and A.J...."

"Yes."

"You said you weren't alone through this whole mess, and I'm glad you weren't, but..."

"She's married," he said, his feelings a closely guarded secret at that moment. "And that's the end of it, as far as I'm concerned."

"But you still...have feelings for her?"

He looked down at the glass of wine in his hand, as if he could find some sort of answer there. He'd been careful to point out to her that this was simply one night. And she wasn't quite sure she could go through with that now.

"I'm sorry," she began. "You don't have to explain, and I shouldn't have asked."

"I don't mind telling you," he said. "I just had to think for a minute. It's a complicated situation, and our relationship worked on a lot of different levels. For a long time, I thought I was *in* love with her. And I do still love her. I'm very proud of her. I'm proud of the work she's doing and all that she's made of her life. I think there will always be a special bond between us, but that's the end of it."

"Oh." Laura could live with that. And she believed what he was saying. After all, there weren't many men who would admit to loving a woman they couldn't have, especially not in the midst of taking another woman to bed.

If indeed he was going to take her to bed.

Laura wasn't sure what she did, what gave her away, but he seemed to know exactly what she was thinking. He took a sip of his wine, and reminded her once again of the devil himself. And he smiled at her. She sometimes thought the world was going to tip on its axis when he smiled.

"A.J. and I never had a sexual relationship," he said.

"Oh." That was certainly a relief.

"We were never more than very good friends," he added.

Which left only one basic question. "And what are you and I?"

"I hope we're going to be lovers, Laura. How would that be? As a start?"

With a trembling hand, she set the wineglass on the counter. "We could start there."

They began with a slow dance and a kiss. Nick found a radio station playing some old jazz and lit a few candles that now burned throughout the apartment. He poured Laura another glass of wine, then pulled her into his arms.

It felt wonderful. Danger seemed so far away.

She felt a little reckless tonight, and at the same time, she felt perfectly safe in his arms.

Laura had expected him to rush her; men always seemed to be in a rush about these things. Relieved that he wasn't, she enjoyed his body as it brushed tantalizingly against hers while they danced in the near darkness of the kitchen.

There was something incredibly seductive about agreeing to make love to this man, then having all this time in anticipation. His hands were warm and slow, moving across her back, down through her hair, then to her hips. They moved more and more slowly to the music, each caress of her breasts against his chest or his thighs against hers making her only want him more.

She never knew it was possible to want a man this much. She swayed closer to him, tightened her grip on his waist, pressed her cheek against his chest, all the while aching for the feel of his lips on her flesh.

"Nick?" she said finally.

"Hmm?"

He nuzzled her ear, his warm breath sending shivers down her spine. The touch had the breath rushing out of her body on a long, low sigh. Goose bumps rose on her skin, leaving her tingling all over.

"No rush, right?"

He spoke the words into her ear, an instant before his mouth settled over this mass of nerves at the side of her neck. Her knees nearly buckled, and she tightened her grip on him as his mouth moved up and down along the side of her neck.

Laura didn't know whether to pull him closer or beg him to stop. The sensations were so intense she didn't think she could stand it. It seemed as if every nerve ending in her body began at that spot in her neck covered by his mouth and ended in the spot at the juncture of her thighs.

One of her hands was tangled in his hair, telling him in no uncertain terms that she liked what he was doing to her neck. They'd given up all pretense of the dance and now he simply rocked his hips against hers, the pressure leaving no doubt about how aroused he was.

"Touch me," he begged, guiding her hand between their bodies.

And then it was his turn to gasp.

"Laura," he warned, "I haven't done this in a very long time."

"Neither have I." She held him through his clothes, cupping him in her hand, wanting him more with each passing second. And she intended to make him want her just as much. "Am I doing something wrong?"

"What do you think?"

"I think you're a tease."

In response, he left a string of slow, soft bites down the side of her neck and across her collarbone. When his mouth passed along the scooped-out neckline of the shirt she wore, finding the curve of her breasts, he started sucking softly against them, until he'd pushed the shirt off one shoulder. His hand came under the shirt, cupping her breast and holding it up, until his mouth could reach it above the neckline of the shirt.

By the time his mouth closed over the tip of her breast and he started laving it with his tongue, Laura would have done anything to have him inside her.

She would have pleaded, cried—anything. He lifted her in his arms. For one dizzying instant, she felt his arousal flush against belly. Then he sat her down on the edge of the counter, stripped her of her panties and started nibbling on her thighs.

Laura gasped in surprise and pleasure so intense she thought she would surely die from it. The pressure deep inside her came on so quickly, so strongly, that it was nearly over before she realized it.

"Wait," she cried. When he looked up at her with his smoky brown eyes, she told him, "I don't want to do this alone. I want you with me."

He was breathing as hard as she was, and he was smiling, too, as he loosened his pants and ripped open the package with the condom. "If you insist."

Laura didn't think she'd ever been so greedy for the touch of a man's body against her own. His mouth went back to the side of her neck, as she pulled him to her. She felt the pressure at the juncture of her thighs again, felt the heat, felt his muscles tense, then heard him groan.

"I'll never be able to make this last for you," he admitted.

"Next time," she murmured. There would be a next time.

He slid inside her in one long, slow, easy thrust, and she wrapped her legs around him to hold him there. He was big and hard and hot, the pressure of his body inside her more intense than anything she'd ever felt.

He rocked his body against hers, holding her hips in the palms of his hands, and she just couldn't get close enough to him, even now.

"Don't stop." Her words came out as no more than a ragged whisper. "Don't."

Still, she knew it was all going to be over soon, that it could never last long enough to satisfy her need for him. Because she needed to do more than make love to this man. She needed much more, needed it desperately.

In the end, she couldn't say how long it lasted; she'd lost all sense of time, all sense of place, until there was nothing but Nick and the sound of her name on his lips, the feel of his body straining against hers.

"Come with me," he implored, knowing she was trying to hold back, to make it last.

She moaned, incapable of putting anything into words just then.

"With me," he insisted, then proceeded to show her that it wasn't up to her anyway, that she couldn't control the reaction of her body to his.

The tension built to the point where she simply couldn't bear it. Her body throbbed to the rhythm of his. Her heart pounded in time with his, and she called out his name as the pleasure rolled over her in long, satisfying waves.

She clung to him with every bit of strength she had left in her body and wished she never had to let go of him. He laughed, a wondrous sound of triumph and sheer happiness unlike anything she'd ever heard from him. This was the old Nick, Laura realized, the one buried under a year's worth of anger and disillusionment. She'd managed to reach him after all.

When she found the strength to lift her head from his shoulder, he was smiling at her in a way that changed his entire face. She put her hand to his cheek, fingered the tiny worry lines around the corners of his eyes that had seemed so pronounced before. Now she saw dimples, too. The man had dimples in his cheeks when he smiled. He looked twice as devastating now, even more the heartbreaker than before.

Laura would swear that this man had broken more than his share of young girls' hearts in his high-school and college days. Would he add hers to the list? She suspected he would, but that wasn't something she was going to let herself worry about right now.

Right now he was hers, and with a strength that amazed her after what they'd just done, he shifted her in his arms, then lifted her and carried her to the sofa in the living room. She was still settling herself against the cushions when he pulled off his pants and followed her down.

He pushed the shirt up around her neck, then took the time to pull it over her head and throw it to the side. She sighed softly as this wondrous heat and weight of a naked, aroused male settled on top of her.

With a killer smile, he told her, "I don't think once is going to be enough, Laura."

Chapter 11

Laura was dozing beside him on the sofa, her body wrapped around his, when sometime early in the morning the phone rang. She was slow to come awake, reluctant to lose this spot beside him or to give up that languorous web of sexual satisfaction that surrounded them.

Nick raised his head and turned in the direction of the sound, but he didn't move until Drew's voice, projected from the answering machine, sent him scrambling for the phone on the end table at the opposite end of the sofa.

He punched a button to stop the machine from broadcasting their conversation, and Laura knew instinctively that reality had just intruded into their too-brief time together.

She sat up and pulled the afghan around her body.

Watching him, she could tell by his body language that he was totally tuned in to the business at hand.

They were all in some sort of trouble. This night, these stolen moments, couldn't last. She wouldn't regret what they had done, only the fact that the problems of the world outside this apartment had impinged so soon.

She'd known this would happen, she just wished they could have a few more days to themselves first.

"What's wrong?" she asked as he replaced the receiver.

Nick turned back to her. In the dim light, she could make out the sleek, powerful lines of his body, and she appreciated fully the set of weights pushed into the corner in the bedroom.

His hair was tousled, his eyes guarded, and he needed to shave. He looked tired, a little unsure of himself and very serious. Laura didn't like it at all.

Nick hesitated a minute, then stretched his right arm along the back of the sofa. "Come a little closer."

He didn't have to ask a second time. She settled herself against his side, shut her eyes for a moment as his arm curled around her. The world wasn't such a cold place after all.

Nick shook his head, worrying her. "I didn't think of this at all."

"What?"

"Late last night, the cops found a body in an alley about a block and a half from Rico's apartment."

"Yes?"

"A young woman's body."

"Oh, no." Laura hadn't thought about that possibility, either.

She waited a minute, letting the news sink in. She'd hated Renata Leone at times. She'd cursed her, damned her, railed to anyone who would listen.

And Laura was jealous of her, because she wanted Rico for her own. She wanted him because she thought she could be a better mother than Renata, and she wanted Rico to have a decent home. But Laura also felt guilty for coveting Renata's son.

Now Renata's poor little boy was asleep in the next room, Laura was taking care of him, and Renata...

"So, she's dead."

Nick shrugged noncommittally. "The cops are waiting on a dental-records check for a positive ID, but Drew seems fairly confident that the body is Renata's."

"Oh, God. All this time...I was so mad at her. I thought she'd just gone off and left him again. I never imagined that she might be dead."

Nick was silent beside her, waiting, watching her, clearly worried.

Tears welled up in Laura's eyes and spilled over, though she made no sound. She had tried to help Renata, then given up on the woman, preferring to concentrate her energy on Rico. Laura didn't understand how any addiction to any kind of drug would be more important than a woman's child, although she had tried to help Renata by getting her in touch with a variety of community-service agencies.

"I should have done more to help her," Laura said, certain of that now. "But I was so angry at her, Nick."

"Hey, you couldn't save her from herself. She was lucky she had you to look after Rico when she was too messed up to do it herself." He took her chin in his hand and forced her to look at him. "You can't help someone who doesn't want to be helped."

"I know, but...oh, God. How are we going to tell Rico this?"

"I don't think we should tell him anything yet. There's no need to upset him any more until we're certain the body is hers."

"He'll be devastated." Laura had already accepted it herself. Renata Leone was dead.

"Laura, if this is his mother's body, I don't think her death is going to come as a surprise to Rico. Remember, when he walked into the shelter he had blood on his shoes and his pants."

"Yes, but . . . ?" Laura didn't see the connection at first. She'd jumped to conclusions. "I just assumed that Renata OD'd. She came so close to doing that before."

Nick shook his head. "She was murdered. Someone slit her throat."

They didn't sleep after that. Laura couldn't. Every time she closed her eyes, she imagined Renata lying there in a pool of blood. Poor Rico. How terrible that night must have been for him.

Laura thought she was going to be sick. Nick made her take a long, cool shower, then wrapped her up in what must have been one of his robes. It was a mile too big, made of heavy terry cloth, but still she was shivering. He held her in his arms until the worst of it passed.

"You're going to help me, aren't you? You'll help me help Rico deal with this?"

"Yes."

"I don't even know where to start."

"Well, let's talk about it. It will give you something to think about, instead of feeling guilty that it's your fault."

"I . . . I just wish I'd done more."

"Think about Rico," he suggested. "You can help Renata best right now by helping him."

"Tell me how."

"When a child loses a parent, one of his first questions is likely who will take care of him now. So, where's his father?"

If Laura knew, she would have strangled the man long ago. "He didn't last very long. He took off sometime before Rico's first birthday."

"And there's been no contact since then?"

"No visitation, no child support, no forwarding address. He just didn't come home one night. Renata had no idea where to find him, and I don't even know his name. I don't even know if the social worker has his name on the case file."

"Okay, what about aunts, uncles, grandparents, cousins? Anyone like that?"

"Oh, yes," Laura said cynically. "I talked to Renata's mother a few hours after I found the apartment wrecked. We had her number in Rico's school files. I called thinking she might know where her daughter and her grandson were. You know what she said to me? She hadn't seen or heard from Renata in nine years, and she'd never even seen Rico. Can you imagine that? He's her grandson."

Nick wrapped his arms tighter around her, and right now it felt as if he were the only thing holding her together.

"I'm sorry," she said, fresh tears flooding her eyes.

He kissed her forehead. "It's all right."

"I just get so angry sometimes."

"We all do, Laura. It's a professional hazard for anyone who works with kids. Tell me about his grandma."

"She kicked Renata out of the house when she found out Renata was pregnant with that 'no-account colored boy's baby.' I told her that her grandson was missing, and she didn't even care. So I can't imagine her stepping forward to take him."

"Great," he said, "so when he asks what's going to happen to him, we'll—"

"Nick." She stopped him. "I want him myself."

He pulled away from her enough that he could see her face. "Permanently?"

"Yes. It nearly killed me when I had to give him up the last time so he could go back home to Renata. I knew something awful was going to happen to him, and I never should have let him go back there."

"Laura, it wasn't your decision to make. And you may want him very much right now, but you have to think about this. It's a very big decision, and you're still trying to get used to the idea that Renata is probably dead."

"I've thought about this for months. I decided after the second time Renata OD'd that if I ever had the chance, I would adopt Rico."

Nick didn't say anything at first.

"I love him very much," she said. "I could never abandon him. He needs me more than ever."

"Do you think you could get permission to adopt him?"

"I'm not sure."

"His father was African-American?"

She nodded.

"You know there's a lot of pressure right now to place black children in black families."

"I know, but his mother was Hispanic, and so am I. Surely that will be enough."

"I hope so, for your sake and for his. But try not to make any promises to him that you're not sure you'll be able to keep, all right? If you tell him that he's going to be your little boy and then the courts won't let you have him, he'll be devastated all over again."

Laura closed her eyes tightly, too easily seeing in her mind someone taking Rico away from her because a judge decided Rico would be better off with someone else.

"I can't lose him," she said. She wouldn't. She and Rico were going to be a family, and Nick . . .

Would Nick be a part of that? Would he want to be a member of their family? She had no idea how he felt about being a father. Working with kids the way he did, she knew he liked them. Surely he wanted children of his own.

She thought briefly of the coldhearted professor in Boston to whom she'd been engaged. She'd mentioned the possibility of adoption to him once, and he'd reacted so coldly to the idea. His children would be his in every way—that precious Boston bloodline of his would run through his children's veins.

Mitch would have never understood, he would have never been able to accept a child like Rico because of the color of Rico's skin alone.

Laura looked at Nick now. He wasn't anything like Mitch. She'd never detected the first bit of prejudice in him.

But Laura wanted to be Rico's mother permanently. She wanted to build a life with him. Rico was a part of her now. If Nick wanted Laura, if he ever came to love her, he'd have to love Rico, as well. She wouldn't settle for less.

After all, the world would always be a difficult place for Rico, merely because of the color of his skin. His own grandmother had rejected him because his father wasn't the same color as she was. Add to that the fact that Rico had never known his father and that his mother had been murdered. He would need every bit of love Laura had to give. He would need a father, also.

What if Nick didn't want to be a father? What if he didn't want to adopt?

"Laura?" he said.

"I'm sorry. I was just thinking. What do I say to Rico?"

"The truth—that you're going to be his foster parent for now while things get sorted out. Let's hope that will be enough to satisfy him initially. Maybe by the time he asks more questions you'll have some answers for him."

"All right." She'd consider that issue settled. As for her and Nick, for families and adoptions, that wasn't something she could let herself think about right now. She still had too many questions about what Renata's murder meant. She thought of one of those remaining questions, the worst one.

"Nick, do you think he saw his own mother die?"

"It would account for the drops of blood on his clothes and his shoes, and it certainly accounts for the fact that he started running and didn't stop for three days, that he hasn't said more than five words since he showed up at the shelter."

"My poor little boy," she said. She'd thought of him that way for the longest time, even though he wasn't hers. "How are we going to explain this to him,

Nick? How are we going to help him? You can help him, can't you?''

He didn't respond, and Laura panicked for an instant before she got her feelings under control. She hadn't made a mistake in putting her faith in this man, she told herself. Surely she wouldn't have made such a monumental mistake.

"I know you can help him," she said, "even if you aren't certain of that yourself."

He looked as if the very idea pained him.

"Nick?"

"I'm going to do everything I possibly can for him."

And then Laura could breathe again.

"I hope that's enough," Nick added.

"It will be. It has to be."

"Honestly, Laura, right now I'm more worried about keeping him alive than anything else."

"Alive?" She hadn't gotten to the point of worrying about that yet. "What else did Drew say?"

"Think about it," Nick said. "What would make Rico so reluctant to talk? Besides seeing his mother that way."

Laura swallowed hard and had to force the words past her lips. "Seeing the man who did it?"

Nick nodded. "Maybe even being warned that there'd be trouble for Rico if he talked about what he saw."

"Oh, no." She tried to deny it for as long as she could.

"I'm afraid so. If Rico saw that man, if he knew that man or he can identify that man, he won't be safe until the man is caught."

Willingly, even gratefully, Laura went back into Nick's arms. She was trembling and cold. Inside her, her heart ached for the little boy sleeping in the next room.

"Laura?" He turned her face toward his again. "In all likelihood you've seen the man, as well. You're in just as much danger as Rico is."

She tried to say something at first, but couldn't. Honestly, she hadn't thought of herself as being in any danger at all, except the danger that came from her proximity to Rico.

And then she considered Nick. "You think the cop who tried to take Rico from the hospital is the one who killed his mother? Rico did say something about him having hurt his mother."

"Him or someone working with him."

"What about you? You saw him, too. So you're in as much danger as Rico or me."

He didn't even blink, didn't hesitate, didn't seem surprised or at all upset by what she'd said. Then he added, "I guess the three of us are in this together."

In this together...

Nick had already come to that conclusion on his own. Even if he hadn't seen the cop that day, there was no way he would bail out on Laura and Rico. They weren't going anywhere without him until this whole mess was over.

Rico had lost his mother; that was difficult enough. If he had indeed seen her body after the murder, then he would need even more help. If he could identify the man who did this to his mother, if that man knew Rico could identify him and had threatened Rico, and if Rico might at some point be called to testify against

that man in court . . . the list went on and on. The boy
would need all the help he could get. Nick was the only
one around right now to help him.

Nick was scared, but he wasn't going to let that stop
him. He'd never been scared before. He'd never been
so unsure of himself or had so little confidence in his
abilities. But one very important thing had come back
to him—the desire to help. That was stronger than ever
before.

He had Rico and the woman now asleep beside him
to thank for that. How did you say thank-you for
something like that? How could he ever explain to her
how much this meant to him? His work had been his
life, and now he wanted the work back. He wanted his
life back.

He wanted the woman sitting beside him. Nick
shifted against her to get one of his hands free. He
took her hands in his, threaded his fingers through
hers, then pressed their palms together.

She was an incredible woman. She had more faith
in her little finger than he had left in his whole body
before she'd come along and shown him what faith
was all about. Curled up against him like this, her
body so familiar, her smell, her touch, he couldn't
believe how much she had changed his life so quickly.

He had a purpose again in life, a reason to get out
of bed, to get out of this apartment. He had a need to
use the skills and the knowledge he carried, knowledge he'd abandoned in the past year. He'd been too
afraid to do that before, afraid that the best he might
have to offer a little boy like Rico wouldn't be good
enough.

This time would be different, he told himself. He would not let Rico down. He wouldn't let Laura down, either.

Maybe he could find a way to thank her properly, if she wanted anything to do with him once this was over.

Nick tried not to think about the possibility that she might not. His life was in a shambles, his career in the toilet, his reputation shot. He didn't even have a job, and he couldn't live off his savings and a few investments forever.

What did he have to offer a woman like Laura?

She deserved a man without any of the emotional baggage he carried, someone who looked at a family as a source of joy and of pride, not someone who'd seen family after family torn apart in every way imaginable. Nick dealt with the ugliness of broken families every day. And then there was his own stellar family background to add to the equation. He thought being a father or a mother had to be the riskiest job of all.

Laura was eager to take on those risks. He doubted she even saw having a family as a risk. Nick could see her with a big house in the suburbs and her and her six kids in a minivan headed for the Little League ball field. He could see her as some very lucky man's reason to come home every night.

And even though he couldn't see himself as a father, he scowled at the thought of some other man rushing home to get to her and her children. He wanted to be that man, but a father to Rico...he broke out in a cold sweat thinking about it.

Then Rico let out his first scream.

Nick ran for the bedroom. Laura wasn't far behind him. He turned on the light, blinding the three of them at first. When he could see again, he knew no one had broken into the apartment. Rico was alone, sitting up screaming in the middle of the double bed.

"It's just a nightmare," Nick said to Laura.

She made her way around him and climbed onto the bed, sitting directly in front of Rico. "Hey, little man, it's all right. Miss Laura is here."

She was right before him, but Rico seemed to stare straight through her. And he was still screaming. Laura took his hand at first, holding it, stroking it, then pulled him into her arms. Rico resisted for a minute, then finally seemed to break free of the nightmare's grip.

"That man..." he said tearfully, "he hurt my mother."

"I know, Rico. But you're with me and Nick now, and we're going to keep that man away from you, okay?"

He gave her a glassy-eyed look, his chin dipping a little lower. He backhanded the tears on one cheek, then the other, and sniffled. "He hurt my mother."

"I know," Laura said, then turned to Nick for guidance. "What do I do now?"

Nick watched her with the boy. Comforting him seemed to come so easily to her. At one time it had come easily to Nick, as well.

"You do exactly what you're doing right now," he whispered back to her, all the while wondering if she even needed him.

Nick left the two of them there on the bed and wandered into the hallway. More than anything right now, Rico needed to feel safe and secure. He needed to know someone was going to take care of him, and that someone was Laura.

Hopefully, soon, he'd be ready to talk to Nick about what had happened. Nick wasn't going to push him on that, not now that he had an idea of how much trauma the child had suffered.

He walked into the living room and stared out the window into the darkness. He had felt safe having the two of them here, but now that he knew there was a murderer on the loose, he wasn't so sure. Above all, he wanted them to be safe until this crazy cop was caught.

Because if anything happened to the two of them, he didn't think he'd survive the aftermath.

Sometime later, the phone rang. Nick looked at his watch; it was shortly before eight. He walked to the answering machine and waited for Drew's voice. When it came, he lifted the receiver and turned off the recorder. "I'm here. What's up?"

"Not much," Drew said. "We're still waiting for the dental-records check. I still have more questions than answers, but I don't like the way this feels. Everybody is pulling ranks on me and clamming up. It shouldn't be this hard to get some information on a dirty cop."

"Which means?" Nick prompted.

"There must be more to this than one dirty cop."

"Great."

"I'd say there's one hell of a big mess somewhere within the police department, and the kid and his mother just happened to get in the middle of it."

Nick couldn't fault the logic in that. He believed in gut feeling, in instinct, and he trusted Drew, which prompted him to add, "Rico is starting to talk again."

"Good. What did he see?"

"I think he saw the guy who slit his mother's throat, although we haven't gotten that far yet."

"What did he say?"

"Just that the man hurt his mother. But the rest of the story is going to come out, I'm sure. He just needs some time."

"So do I. And I think it's time for the three of you to get out of town. How do you all feel about taking a little trip?"

"Point the way," Nick said.

"I don't have any particular direction in mind just yet. I'm not even working on this officially."

"Okay."

"Give me a few hours to arrange it. I've been up all night trying to cut through this mountain of a bureaucracy surrounding this mess. But I have friends in lots of out-of-the-way places. I'll find you a spot. Pack your things and be ready to move this morning. Let's say ten o'clock, all right?"

"That's fine."

"Don't open the door for anyone but me."

"I won't. And, Drew, I appreciate it."

"Anytime, my friend. By the way, Carolyn wants to know if you're coming out of retirement. She's ready to put you back to work at the shelter."

"Which means she needs someone who works cheap."

"That's part of it," he admitted. "But she's been worried about you."

"So have I. Tell her we'll talk when this mess is all over."

Nick found Laura asleep on the bed, with Rico's head on her shoulder. He let the two of them sleep until nine, so they had time to get ready before Drew arrived.

Rico was silent again. Laura was quiet, as well. Nick wondered whether she was uncomfortable around him because they had made love the night before, or whether she was frightened because Drew thought they needed to leave town.

A part of him ached to take her in his arms and hold her close, to tell her that he was here and that he would do everything in his power to keep her safe. And another part of him wondered what she would do if he tried to pull her close.

Now that morning had come, did she regret what had happened between them? Nick was sure sex was something she didn't take lightly.

He wanted to tell her that the night meant a great deal to him, that she meant a great deal to him, too. But he wasn't sure he could put into words the feelings he didn't understand that well himself yet.

He wanted her again. He wanted to make her smile, to be the kind of man with whom she'd want to be involved. He had a ways to go on that score, and he didn't think he was in a position to make her any promises, because he wouldn't make promises right now.

Laura deserved much better than him. Maybe that was the real problem—he didn't think he deserved a woman like her. So he kept his distance that morning.

The three of them moved around the apartment like polite strangers. Rico ate a little. Laura didn't have anything. They both showered and dressed, then waited for Drew to knock on the door.

At three minutes to ten, Laura thought she heard something out front.

"What kind of a sound?" Nick headed for the window, motioning for her to stay back.

"I'm not sure."

And there it was again, a popping that reverberated off the walls. Nick pushed the shades aside and saw a lot of people running in different directions on the sidewalk below. They were yelling and gesturing back toward the front of the building. He backtracked, then picked out a man in a dark suit with a gun in his hand.

FBI, he thought. He doubted many crooks wore dark suits on the job.

Nick's gaze swept over the area again, and he still didn't see Drew. But Drew was down there. Nick was certain that if Drew Delaney said he'd be here at ten, he would. So who knew Drew was going to be here and who was waiting for him when he arrived?

Nick was certain they also knew Rico was up here. He didn't have time right now to figure out how someone could know that, because he intended to make sure the men downstairs shooting didn't find Rico up here.

"It's gunfire, isn't it?" Laura asked softly.

Nick turned and looked down into her frightened eyes, wishing it were anything but the sound of a gun, then nodded gravely.

"What are we going to do?"

He hesitated for one second, maybe two. Someone was likely going to come to his apartment at any minute. Nick didn't want to be in here wondering who was on the other side of the door when that happened. "We're going to get out of here. How do you feel about heights?"

She paled.

"We're only on the fourth floor."

"Only?"

"The fire escape is this way. We'll end up in the alley in back." He knew because he'd worried that one day when his case finally came to trial the reporters would find him and hold him captive in his own apartment, so he'd checked out the fire escape. He'd never thought he would end up leaving that way because of some crazy man with a gun.

Laura still looked skeptical.

"We're sure not going out the front door," he said.

"I know, but..." She glanced back at Rico, who looked as frightened as she did.

"Laura, I don't want to wait until someone shows up at the door to see whether they blast through it or knock and flash an FBI ID. Either way, we wouldn't know whether we could trust them unless it was Drew himself."

"I know, but..." She closed her eyes and made a desperate grab for air.

Nick didn't think they had the time to waste, but he couldn't bear the expression in her eyes. He took a few precious minutes to pull her into his arms and hold her tight.

"Listen to me," he insisted. "Whoever is down there is going to have to go through me to get to Rico or to you."

That part was nonnegotiable. Maybe this whole relationship wasn't as complicated as he thought. He'd found his bottom line fast when the shooting started.

"I'm not going to lose you now, Laura. So get moving. Grab that tote bag you packed and follow me."

They battled with the window, the frame either swollen or painted shut, then made it onto the rusty railings and ladders of the fire escape. The structure creaked ominously as it took the weight of the three of them. The wind howled through the tall buildings. Rico clung to Nick as if he'd never let go. The boy hardly weighed anything, and his arms were so skinny the strength in them amazed Nick. He hoped he was doing the right thing to deserve such faith from the trembling little boy.

From the front of the building, they heard shouts and nervous screams, but no more gunfire. A quick check of the alley showed nothing but frightened people still running past on the main road in front. In the distance, the sirens howled. Behind Nick, Laura lost her footing and gave a muffled scream. Nick took a second to steady her on her feet, then give her a fast, hard kiss on the mouth.

"I'm not going to lose you now," he repeated.

Then he headed down the last flight. He pried Rico's hands from around his neck, then waited for the boy to grab onto the ladder. Laura worked her way down beside Rico and started reassuring him. Nick jumped to the ground—a drop of about six feet—then glanced around again. As far as he could tell, the alley was still empty. Maybe their luck would hold.

"Okay, Laura, he's going to have to jump."

Rico shook his head. Nick heard him sobbing now. Laura said something to him. Rico finally looked down. Nick held up his arms, and the boy leaped into them.

Once again, skinny little arms clamped around his neck with surprising strength. A head covered with dark, tight curls came down against his chest. Nick closed his eyes and started to pray as he hadn't in years, then looked up at Laura.

He tried not to think about how frightened she appeared at this moment or how vulnerable she'd been the night before. There'd be time to reassure her later. Somehow he'd make time for them. For now, they had to move.

"Jump," he told her. And she did, landing hard beside him. Then the three of them took off running.

They didn't look back until they stopped at an ATM at a busy street corner three blocks down. If they were going to get out of town, they needed cash. Nick didn't want to wait too long to get it, in case someone had the power to track transactions in his bank accounts. So they stopped while they were still in the middle of town, then bypassed two train stations before taking the third.

Once they were on the train, they just rode as far as it would take them toward the north side of town, where they rented a car from a place that didn't care if Nick claimed he had no credit card. And then they tried their best simply to disappear.

Chapter 12

They drove half the day and into the night, stopping only long enough to grab something to eat and find pay phones from which to call Drew Delaney.

Nick was starting to get worried by early evening when he hadn't been able to reach Drew. The people in Drew's office gave him all sorts of excuses about why he couldn't speak to Drew, and Nick didn't believe any of them.

A lot of shots were fired that morning in front of the building, and he was starting to fear the worst. If one of those bullets got Drew, Nick didn't know what he'd do next. He liked Drew; he knew his wife, knew they had an older son and a brand-new baby. And Drew was a good agent. No one deserved to be gunned down on the job, but especially not a man like Drew.

Nick had to think of Rico and Laura now, too. If Drew wasn't able to guide them through this mess, Nick wasn't sure who he could turn to for help, especially if there were a bunch of dirty cops and FBI agents in town.

Finally, around nine that night, he managed to get through to Drew at the agent's office. The news wasn't good. Not good at all. After about fifteen minutes on the phone with Drew, Nick hung up and started driving again.

They stopped at a big discount store around ten and Laura drove around the parking lot in circles while Nick went in to buy toothbrushes, toothpaste, shampoo, necessities like that. Wherever they were going, they needed to be prepared to stay an indefinite period of time.

Around eleven, they found a run-down motel on the lake with some cabins in the woods farther from the shore. Nick chose it because he thought he could rent one without using a credit card or pulling out some ID. He made Rico stay in the car, out of sight, letting the woman who rented him the cabin think he and Laura were alone.

Rico didn't even wake up when Nick carried him into the back bedroom. The little boy had been silent most of the day, once he calmed down after they escaped from the apartment. The gunfire had scared him. The man who hurt his mother had a gun, he told them. Laura wondered if the man also had a knife, one he'd used to cut Renata Leone's throat.

She tucked Rico into the half bed in the back room, kissed his cheek and made him a half-dozen promises she hoped to be able to keep.

He would ask soon about his mother, and Laura still had to figure out what she was going to tell him. She understood Nick's reasoning in wanting to wait until they knew for certain the dead woman was Renata Leone, but Nick also believed Rico had seen the murderer, possibly even the murder. So Laura had to be prepared for anything he might ask.

One question would be easy to answer. When he asked who would take care of him now, she would tell him of her plans to adopt him.

Of course, she had the child-welfare people to contend with, but she didn't think they would give her any trouble. After all, people had never lined up to adopt troubled eight-year-old boys of mixed race.

Laura heard a sound at the doorway to the bedroom and turned toward it. Nick was standing there watching her.

"Is he all right?"

Laura nodded, stood and walked to him. One of his big, strong hands took hold of hers, the touch setting off all sorts of sparks inside her. She didn't want to give up Nick, either, and she wondered what her chances were of getting to keep him, as well.

She told herself that she needed to be prepared to lose him.

During those tense moments outside Nick's apartment on the fire escape, with the gunfire below them, he had told her in no uncertain terms that he wasn't going to lose her yet. Laura had hoped for some sort of a miracle. She'd imagined her and Nick and Rico together in half a dozen different places and times, and she'd started dreaming in earnest of a future with Nick.

But now that she had time to think about it, her own insecurities had grown with each passing minute. She wasn't daydreaming now. She was seeing him return to the life he used to live, especially if helping Rico handle his mother's murder also managed to help Nick work through the trauma that had followed Jason Williams's death.

Nick would go back to his psychiatry practice. Laura would go back to teaching her second graders at Saint Anne's and making a life for herself and Rico. She didn't see her and Nick crossing paths again.

The thought of never seeing him anymore brought sudden tears to her eyes. Nick noticed, and wiped the first one away before it even made its way down her cheek.

"Are you all right?" he asked.

His voice alone was enough to send a shiver of awareness down her spine. "I've had better days," she admitted.

"Me, too."

He left his hand on her cheek. Laura thought for a minute he was going to kiss her again and wished he would. She wondered what the women he knew were like. When he dated, what sort of women did he choose?

There was a whole world out there of money and privilege and places in society about which she knew nothing. And at times she would have said those things didn't matter at all to Dr. Nicholas Garrett. But then some of her old insecurities would rise up.

She'd gone to school on some miraculous scholarship that she thought would change her life forever. But she never felt she fit in there, although she'd tried hard with Mitch and his blue-blooded Boston family. Whether it was the fact that she was poor, that her skin was darker than theirs, that her family had been in this country for only sixty years or so compared with the almost four hundred years his family had been here, she would never know. They hadn't explained their instant dislike of her or their vehement objections to Mitch's involvement with her.

But she'd felt it as distinctly as the touch of someone's hand on hers. They hadn't wanted her. They would never accept her.

Laura knew next to nothing about Nick's family or his background. Or if he even had a family.

Would she fit in his life once this whole mess was over?

She didn't know. But she did know one thing. She and Nick were together now, and she intended to make the most of that time.

She smiled up at him and kept her tears at bay. Some emotion flared to life in his eyes, and his gaze settled once again on her lips.

The wait seemed to go on forever, and she couldn't understand why he would be hesitating now, after they had already made love the night before at his apartment. She was about to ask him why, about to make the first move herself, when his hand fell away from her cheek and he stepped back.

His withdrawal hurt, more than she cared to think about right now. Laura forced her mind back to the business at hand and chided herself for ever losing sight of it.

"Are you ready yet to tell me what's going on?" she asked briskly.

He hadn't wanted to say much earlier in front of Rico. But hours had passed since he talked to Drew. She'd had time to imagine any number of terrible things that could have gone wrong.

"Come this way," he told her, motioning her out of the room. "Come outside with me. It's a beautiful night."

Laura closed the bedroom door behind her, then walked through the small combination living room and kitchen and out the front door.

They were in the middle of nowhere, in a stand of tall, thick trees somewhere near the lake. There were no sounds of cars, no sirens, no clicking noise of a train rushing past. There were no people shouting or singing or cursing anywhere nearby. It was eerily silent, save for the crickets chirping and the frogs croaking. And to a city girl like her, used to the bright lights, it was incredibly dark out here.

Nick walked to the side of the car and leaned against it. He crossed his arms in front of him and watched her with the kind of intensity that had the power to make her mouth go dry and to make her forget how afraid she was and how certain she was that she would lose Nick someday.

Maybe she'd already lost him. Maybe that one night was all they would ever have.

Laura shook her head. "Tell me what Drew had to say. Was he at the apartment building today? Were those men after us?"

Nick nodded. "It's more of a mess than we realized."

She had guessed that. "And Rico is right in the middle of it."

"The three of us, Laura. We're all in the middle of this mess together. Renata Leone's boyfriend is part of some ring of cops who've been 'skimming' for a long time now."

"Skimming?"

"Helping themselves to some things they shouldn't. Cops take lots of things as evidence—cash, drugs, stolen property. You name it—you can probably find it in a police station evidence room. Sometimes they get greedy.

"Think about it. A couple of cops who put their lives on the line day in and day out for pay that's laughable find themselves sitting in a house with a man with a record a mile long. He's got a suitcase full of cash right there in front of them or a cache of drugs with some astronomical street value. Who's going to know, at that point, if some of it doesn't make it to the station with him?

"They skim some of the cash or some of the drugs off the top, either before it's booked into evidence or sometimes after it is. Pretty soon the cops are more dangerous than the crooks they're on the streets to catch."

Laura closed her eyes and thought about how dangerous such a man could be once he turned his back on the law but still had all the connections and all the power of a law-enforcement officer. "That's what Renata's boyfriend was doing?"

"Her boyfriend and a number of others. Drew doesn't know how many yet. The cops don't know. And it's damned hard to investigate when the people doing the investigating might be involved in the crime itself. Now someone's facing a murder charge, too. They're more desperate to cover their tracks and silence that little boy than they ever were, to the point of bringing this out into the open by shooting on a public street in the middle of the morning.

"It's a very dangerous situation, and honestly, I don't know what we should do next."

Laura felt sickened by it all. "I thought we were going to stay here. Surely we're safe here."

"We thought we were safe in my apartment, too, and they found us there."

"How? How did they find us? No one knew we were there."

"Drew did. And when he started trying to find some information on Renata's boyfriend, he made the people investigating the skimming operation very nervous. He had to tell a few people why he was asking so many questions."

"Oh." She thought she understood finally.

"Exactly. Someone he told, either someone within the FBI or the police department, came after us. They either heard from Drew or from one of his superiors talking about us. Then they found out where we were. Drew said the dirty cops must be half-crazy to start shooting like that on the street."

"Nobody caught those men outside the apartment building this morning?"

"No. Drew didn't come expecting a shoot-out in public, and he didn't want to tell too many people where we were. So it was just him and his partner."

"They're okay?"

"They are." He paused.

"And Drew thinks they've ID'd one of the gunmen outside the apartment. Still, the FBI and the police have no idea who the top man might be, or how high up he might be in either organization. And now Drew doesn't know who we can trust for help in this."

Laura looked around her at the thick trees, the clouds above that blocked out the moonlight. Were they safe here? Would they be safe anywhere until these men were caught?

"There's one more thing," Nick said. "The dental records check out. Rico's mother is dead."

"Oh." Laura put her hand over her mouth and concentrated on breathing in and out. She looked back toward the cabin, where the little boy lay sleeping, and she ached for him.

Nick took her hand, and she held on to him tightly.

"I thought I was prepared for that, and now that it's happened . . ."

"It's okay."

He took her other hand, as well, in a grip that helped to steady her.

"Oh, God, now I have to tell him."

"I'll help you," he said.

"I don't know how I'm going to tell him. I . . . I still remember when my uncle came to tell me my mother was dead, and it's absolutely the worst thing in the world."

"He's going to get through it, Laura."

She was still having trouble believing this. "Is your mother alive?"

He nodded. "She'll probably live to be ninety. She's indestructible."

"I was five years older than Rico is now when I lost my mother, and it was . . . devastating. It was like no pain I've ever experienced, and there's nothing that makes you feel more alone in this world. You've lost the one person who was always supposed to understand you and forgive you and love you, no matter what. And I . . . I hate that he has to go through that. I hate it, and it makes me so mad."

"Hey," Nick said. "Rico didn't have that kind of a mother."

"Still, she was his mother."

"I know, but he's going to have you. Laura, you'll be the mother he never had. You'll be the one who'll understand him and forgive and love him, no matter what. He may not realize it right now, but he's a damned lucky kid. Don't you forget that."

"I hope you're right."

"Hey, look what an amazing woman you turned out to be."

He kissed her lightly on the lips and wiped away her tears.

Laura would have stayed there in his arms indefinitely, but he dropped his hands and stepped back.

"We've got some other things we have to talk about first," he said.

First? She wondered what would come after the talk. "What are we going to do?" she asked.

"I don't know."

"What did Drew suggest?"

"He said he can put us in touch with another agent in another town, if we'd like to go to some sort of FBI safe house. But that would involve getting back on the road, back into the open for a while."

"I don't want to do that." She'd been terrified all day. So had Rico. "Drew could send someone to get us, couldn't he?"

"If we wanted to tell him where we are. If we were willing to count on the fact that no one has managed to tap his phone or trace calls coming into his phone. We know the murderer has keyed in on Drew, that he knew where we were today, and he'll likely know where we are now."

"We've put Drew in a very dangerous position," she said.

"He's been in dangerous spots before. He can cover his backside."

"You still didn't tell me—do you think we're safe here? Should we stay?"

"Well, Drew wouldn't let me tell him where we are, so a phone tap wouldn't have done anyone any good if they were listening in on the conversation. We didn't use a credit card at all, so there's nothing to track that way. We're traveling in a rental car. I'd say, unless someone managed to follow us from the apartment this morning we're safe as long as we stay put here. What do you think?"

"I feel safer here than I did when we were out in the open today."

"So you want to stay?"

She hedged. "Do you?"

"I'd feel a lot better right now if I were an FBI agent instead of a psychiatrist."

"Rico needs a psychiatrist, though."

"I think he needs both, Laura. I know you need someone like Drew right now much more than you need me."

She fought the urge to tell him just how much she wanted to be with him, no matter what the circumstances.

Nick came toward her then. One minute he was in the shadows, dark hair, dark brooding eyes, broad shoulders, soft lips, and the next minute he walked into the light shining from the fixture above the cabin door.

With the lines sharply etched into the corners of his eyes and his mouth he looked exhausted. She wondered if he'd slept at all the night before, because when she'd woken up he was already up and dressed.

Standing directly in front of her, he hesitated for the time it took her to draw one shaky breath. Then his hands enveloped one of hers. He ran his thumb over the back of her hand and squeezed it.

"If anything happened to Rico or to you because of something I did . . . I don't know what I'd do."

"I'm not going to let anything happen to him. I promised him that. You made me a promise, too, when we were on the fire escape. You said..." She lost all her nerve then, but somehow found it again. "You said you weren't going to lose me now."

He looked off to the right and avoided her gaze. "And you want to know what that means?"

She nodded, her voice gone.

Nick's lips closed over hers, his kiss fast, hard, hungry, just enough to make her want more. Would she always end up wanting more than she got from this man?

"Can it mean that?" he asked as he pulled away just as quickly. "Can it simply mean that I want you and that I'd never forgive myself if anything happened to you now?"

She supposed it could easily mean that. Anything more meaningful was obviously out of the question right now—at least as far as Nick was concerned.

Laura would have to accept that, to try not to let it hurt her, try not to put too much meaning into it right now. After all, there was some crazy man with a gun after them.

"All right," she said. "I want to stay here. For now."

He held on to her hand one more minute, then, with something she hoped was reluctance, let it go.

"In the morning, I'll drive into the little town we passed about five miles back, tell Drew what we're going to do and pick up some food to stock the kitchen. We'll stay put until something breaks in Chicago."

Nick stood outside with Laura, looking at the stars and not speaking, once they'd made their decision to stay at the cabin for the time being.

He wasn't sure what to say or what to do. But he knew what he wanted: he wanted Laura beside him in that little bed in the second bedroom of the cabin. He wanted her right now. In fact, he'd wanted her all day, all through the night before, ever since the moment she'd left him after the second time they'd made love.

For the hundredth time in the past hour or so, he asked himself what he had to offer a woman like Laura. He asked himself what she might want in a man, what she would want for her future and for Rico, the child she planned to adopt. He was sure she would be a wonderful single parent, but that couldn't be her first preference in raising a child.

Children needed a father as well as a mother. He wondered if she had one in mind. Fool that he was, he hadn't even asked if there was some man in her life. And he wanted to know.

"What are you scowling about?" she asked teasingly. "It's absolutely beautiful out here, and you look like you're ready to murder someone.

"I hope it doesn't come to that."

"Nick, what are you talking about?"

He shook his head. "I was just thinking of . . . some unfinished business between us."

"Oh."

She sounded as hesitant as he felt right now.

"You told me about this idiot psychiatry professor you almost married, but that had to be years ago. And we got sidetracked before I could ask about anyone else. What about it, Laura? Is there some other man in your life right now? Is someone waiting for you to get home and worrying about whether you're safe?"

"No. There's no one."

He smiled then. "Good."

"Is that good?" She was being a flirt.

"Yes, I think that's very good."

"Why?"

She was going to make him say it. "Because I might have to hurt the man."

"Oh."

As her mouth opened and the soft word came out, Nick pulled her to him and covered her mouth with his. Kissing her was every bit as sweet as he remembered. The flaming heat still startled him. It began low in his belly, and worked its way outward until it enveloped every inch of his body. He never wanted the connection to end; he wanted to kiss her over and over again until he held nearly the full weight of her body in his arms, until she was boneless and breathless, his to do with as he pleased.

He intended to be very pleased. And he would please her as well.

"Those hours we spent together at my apartment weren't nearly enough," he said, his lips tangled in her hair near her right ear.

"I know."

"Come inside with me, Laura."

"All right."

If she hesitated in the least, he was prepared to be totally honest with her. If she wanted promises, he couldn't give them to her. If she wanted to talk about the future, he'd tell her that he wanted a lot of things for their future, but he couldn't guarantee they would ever come true.

He had to get his life together first. He had to see if he could salvage something of his career—either that or find some new one. He had to face the outside world again, particularly the professional circles in which he moved, and put the disastrous situation with Carter Barnes behind him, once and for all.

And there was her plan to adopt Rico...

He couldn't make any promises to Laura at all.

But she hadn't asked, so he didn't have to say any of those things to her. She'd come into his arms, as hungry for him as he was for her, and Nick felt like the luckiest man in the world right now.

"I don't deserve you," he told her when they made it to the bedroom and he clicked out the light.

Laura sighed heavily and put her arms around him. "You know, I wouldn't call myself an experienced woman by any means, but I haven't lived like a nun, either. I've dated off and on over the years. I've met a lot of men. I've turned a lot of them down. I think you're a prize, Dr. Garrett."

He laughed out loud at that.

"I do."

"Laura—"

"You're kind. You can be very gentle. You genuinely care about people, especially the kids you work with. You're smart and funny and honest. What more would a woman want in a man?"

"Someone who said he loved you?"

"I'd rather have a man who made me *feel* loved than one who simply gave me the words. And I can wait for those words, because I want to know that once he says he loves me, he doesn't have any more doubts, about anything."

Nick put his hand in her hair. He brought it to his face, took in the smell of it, then kissed the side of her head. "You could want someone who has more than a few nights to offer you. Someone ready to make a commitment to you."

"That would be nice—someday. But I don't have to have those things right this minute, either. Why don't you tell me what you can offer me, Nick?"

"I don't think I've ever ached for a woman the way I ache for you."

She smiled then. "That's definitely a very good start."

Nick caught himself thinking too much then. He thought she was one of the most generous women he'd ever met, that she probably spent her whole life giving of herself to the people around her and getting little back in return, taking little back for herself.

And here he was, taking more from her than he had to give back. What did he even have to give her in return?

"You know," he began, "you've changed me. For the first time in a long time, I want someone to believe in me again. I want someone to trust me, to have faith in me."

"I trust you. I have faith."

He kissed her softly in the darkness. "I know, sweetheart. I think you dragged me back to the land of the living, because for the first time in nearly a year,

I want to put my life back together again, and I have you to thank for that.''

He felt tears on her cheeks then, and he felt a heaviness in his heart, a fullness, a warmth. Emotions came rushing at him, making him crush her to him as if he would never let go.

''I'll never be able to show you or to tell you how much you've helped me, and...hey, don't cry. Not now.''

He helped her dry her tears, brushed them away from those long lashes of hers and from the softness of her cheeks.

She kissed him lightly on the lips.

He swore softly and kissed her back, then hesitated once again. With every fiber of his being, he wanted her. He wanted to feel the satiny touch of her bare skin against his, wanted to bury himself inside her.

But there were things he should tell her, things she had a right to know. ''Laura, I care about you a great deal.''

''I know that.'' She touched her fingertips to his lips to silence him. ''And I'm not asking for a string of promises from you tonight, all right?''

He hesitated. It wouldn't be fair to her, but he wanted her so much. She wanted him, as well. They might never have another night like this to be together.

''Nick, it doesn't have to be that complicated right now. I know what's between us.''

''What? Tell me. Because I'm having a devil of a time figuring it out myself.''

''I want to be with you. I want you to kiss me and make me warm all over, tie my stomach into knots and take the breath right out of my body.''

"I think I could do that."

"I know you could."

"But . . ."

"No 'buts.' Not tonight."

And then he kissed her. He devoured her with his mouth and his hands and his body, stripping her of her clothes in seconds flat, shedding his own, pulling her down to the bed beside him.

It had been only hours since they'd made love for the first time, and yet it seemed like forever. He wanted her so badly, took her in this wild flurry of white-hot heat, teasing her relentlessly, bringing her right to the brink of satisfaction and then pulling back again, until he thought he might die from the pleasure of it.

Later, when they made love once more, tenderly this time, with agonizing slowness, he told her, "I'll never get enough of you. Never."

"Careful," she told him back as she rested her head on his shoulder. "You said no promises, and that sounds distinctly like a promise."

"That's definitely a promise, one I'm absolutely certain I can keep. I will never be able to get enough of you."

With that, he made exquisite love to her again. And even that wasn't enough for him.

Chapter 13

Laura awoke to the sight of a dark-haired, dark-eyed man bending over her and calling her name. She sat up quickly, looked around to see Rico sleeping, peacefully at last, beside her in the double bed, then realized what had happened.

In his nightmares the night before, Rico had screamed and cried out for both his mother and for Laura. She'd ended up falling asleep beside him the last time she'd come into the bedroom to comfort him.

Laura rubbed at her eyes, still trying to adjust to the light and to the fact that it was obviously morning and Nick was here.

"What time is it?" she asked. "Is something wrong?"

"No, I haven't seen anyone or heard anything. But it's almost seven, and I want to get into town and back early."

"Okay," she said, still nervous about the prospect of being alone there with Rico.

"I'll hurry," he promised.

"I know."

They had talked last night and agreed that it would be safer to keep Rico out of sight as much as possible, even if that meant leaving him alone with Laura while Nick went into town.

"You can both come with me, if you want. It's not too late to change your mind," he said.

"No. I think it's better this way. It's safer. I just... I'm being silly."

And missing him already. And worrying about him and wishing she hadn't fallen asleep sometime in the middle of the night and lost out on precious hours she could have spent with him.

She wondered if he regretted it, as well. She hated telling Nick goodbye.

"Come in the other room with me for a minute," he said.

Laura climbed out of bed and followed him. "Do you think we'll ever get to spend one whole night together? Or make love in a real bed?"

She thought that would get a smile out of him, hopefully even a kiss, but he looked deadly serious.

"I didn't sleep much last night—it gave me some time to think. Would you answer one more question I have no right to ask?"

"All right."

"I've been thinking a lot about what you said yesterday—that you want to adopt Rico."

"Yes."

"I've been thinking that you'll want him to have a father."

"Yes." Laura made one more attempt to lighten the mood. "Is this some sort of offer?"

He sighed, then cupped her cheeks with his palms, rested his forehead against hers and gazed into her eyes. Laura knew. This was no offer. This was something else entirely.

"He's a great kid," Nick said.

"I know."

"He's lucky that he'll have you for a mother. But he deserves a father, also."

"I want that for him, but I'm not going to run out and marry the first man I find because I think Rico deserves a father. When I marry, I'll do it because I'm in love and because the man I marry loves Rico, as well."

For the life of her, Laura couldn't figure out what this was about. But it frightened her.

Nick looked grim. His hands fell away from her face, and he straightened.

"I care about him a great deal, and I care about you."

"I know."

"Laura, I like kids. I work with them every day. But that doesn't mean..." He stopped, his complexion chalky. "I had a lousy childhood, a lousy father. And I think raising children is one of the hardest and riskiest jobs anyone could take on. In my profession, I've seen families torn apart in every way imaginable."

"I know, but it doesn't always turn out like that," she argued, sensing that she was arguing for her future here, hers and Rico's and Nick's.

"More often than not it does. You know I'm right about this."

"No."

"And you're starting out with so many strikes against you. Rico in all likelihood saw his own mother murdered. In the time she raised him, she abused drugs, she went off for days on end and left him and she had to relinquish him to foster care because she couldn't take care of him herself. And he's never had a father."

"Which means he needs me even more. He deserves so much more than he's ever had."

"I know that."

"So what are you trying to tell me, Nick?"

"That I know what you and that little boy deserve, and I don't think I can be the man to give it to you. I could be a husband to you, but I don't know if I can be a father."

"You don't want to be Rico's father?"

"I don't think I'm cut out to be any kid's father."

Laura bit down hard on her bottom lip, and the pain didn't diminish the one in her heart. "Are you telling me I'll have to make a choice between the two of you?"

"No."

"Because if you are . . ." It would break her heart.

"I'm just trying to be honest with you. I know what you want, and I don't think I can give that to you."

"I think there are a lot of things you aren't telling me." She wished she'd asked a lot more questions of him, about his childhood and his father.

"There are a lot of things you don't know about me," he admitted. "I don't think we have time to get into them right now."

Laura nodded, holding herself as tightly under control as possible.

"I should have told you last night, once I knew Renata was dead," he said.

She nodded.

Nick swore. "I need to get out of here. I wanted to get in and out of town early."

"This isn't over," she insisted.

"I didn't say that it was."

"I'm not giving up on you this easily."

He paused for a moment. "I was hoping you wouldn't."

Laura thought he might try to kiss her again, but he didn't. Instead he said, "I don't want to leave either one of you right now."

She was ridiculously happy to hear it. "Go ahead," she told him, while she was still willing to let him go. "Be careful. And hurry back."

"I will."

Once she had some control over her emotions, Laura took a quick shower, then dressed in a pair of shorts and one of Nick's button-down shirts because she wanted something of his to wrap around her body today. She rolled up the sleeves and tied the ends in a knot at her waist so they didn't hang halfway down her thighs. And then she waited by the window, watching and wondering when he would be back.

She was certain there were a lot of things he hadn't told her, and she would make him tell her someday. Now that she had managed to calm down and think with as much objectivity as she could muster, she didn't believe what Nick *had* told her.

She could see him being a wonderful father, and if he couldn't see that in himself, she would have to show him.

Rico woke up a few minutes later. He was disoriented at first and still calling for his mother.

Laura fed him, let him grumble all the way through his bath, then dressed him in some of the new clothes Nick had bought yesterday when they'd stopped.

Rico still looked sad, but he was losing that dazed expression he'd had at the shelter and in the hospital. He was starting to resemble the little boy she knew and loved.

Maybe he was ready to pull out of this self-imposed silence of his. Nick thought he was, and he'd talked to her last night about some simple things she could do to help Rico.

Nick would work with him, as well, but he thought Laura could do a lot, particularly because with children therapy often looked a lot like play. And Rico was used to spending time playing games and doing art projects with Laura.

"You know what?" she said to the boy. "Nick bought some other things for us, too."

She pulled a plastic bag from the shelf and sat it on the kitchen table in front of him. She found crayons, markers, paints, brushes, construction paper and clay.

"I thought you might like to make something. You can pick whatever you want to use, all right?"

Rico stared at the materials and didn't move at first. Laura had been advised not to make a big deal out of this, so she started straightening up the cabin.

Eventually, Rico picked up the markers and a piece of paper and started to draw.

He made a monster, a huge, ugly, fire-breathing monster, and he appeared angry when he was done. Laura thought Nick would have been pleased. Anger was a very healthy emotion, he claimed. And he should know; he'd spent the past year bottling up an incredible amount of anger.

Laura put the picture down in front of her, then sat on the chair next to Rico.

"That's a pretty scary monster," she said as casually as she could manage.

Rico nodded.

"Can you tell me about the monster?"

He didn't say anything, though his eyes filled with tears. Laura pulled him onto her lap and held him close.

"I hate him," Rico sobbed.

"Why, little man? Why do you hate him?"

"I just do."

"Can you tell me who the monster is?"

"No."

"Does he have a name?"

He nodded.

"Do you know his name?"

Rico continued sobbing. He knew the name of the monster, but he wasn't going to tell her right now.

Laura wiped away some more tears and wished Nick were back. She tried one more thing. "Rico, are you scared of the monster?"

He nodded vigorously.

"Well, you know I'm here now. And Nick will be back soon. That monster would have to get through us to get to you now, and I don't think he could do that. Did you ever think of it that way?"

"No."

"It's true. I'd fight all sorts of fire-breathing monsters for you, little man."

Rico looked a little better. Laura smiled at him and ruffled his hair.

"Now, why don't you draw me another picture?"

Laura went back to stand by the front window of the cabin and watch for Nick.

Nick hadn't been gone that long, when Laura heard a car approaching. She turned cautiously toward the window that looked over the dirt road leading to their cabin. Nick had rented the final cabin on this road. The road ended here. If the car was coming down that road and it was too soon for Nick to return, then whoever was in that car was either coming here or he was lost.

Laura wondered what the chances were of someone ending up lost here in the middle of nowhere near this tiny town and weighed those against the possibility that someone had followed them yesterday when they'd fled from Chicago.

She and Nick had talked it through. No one knew where they were. No one had any way to trace their whereabouts, unless they were followed from the time they'd left Nick's apartment.

It sounded so reasonable when Nick was there. Right now, Laura knew the odds were in their favor—that no one had followed them—but that didn't make her feel any better as the car rumbled down the dirt road through the trees.

"Rico," she called urgently but softly as she scrambled inside the cabin in search of him. "Rico!"

She looked outside, saw a flash of white and black moving through the woods, then went back to her search.

The fear settled heavily into her limbs. It sent her heart rate soaring and made it difficult for her to think. She tried desperately to calm herself, because she had to think. She had to find Rico and get him out of there. Hopefully, Nick would be back soon—

And then she put the next piece of the puzzle together. If the cop had followed them, he might have found Nick already, since he'd left this morning.

Laura froze for a moment, Nick's face flashing before her eyes; something that felt irrationally like love, the kind that came in a blinding light, settled heavily deep in her heart.

She did love him, even if she'd known him for only five days.

And five days wasn't nearly enough for two people in love.

Nick wasn't dead, Laura told herself. This cop hadn't killed him, as he'd killed Rico's mother. Laura had to believe that or she wouldn't be able to go on.

"Rico!" She yelled that time. One frightened little boy stood up from his spot in the corner by the fridge. "Come on. We have to go."

They ran out the door and slammed it behind them. Laura wished she'd remembered to grab some of their things, like the wallet that held some cash Nick had given her, along with phone numbers for Drew Delaney, in case they ever got separated.

But it was too late now. There was no time.

They ran behind the biggest tree Laura saw, then tried to remain absolutely still. Rico was frightened, but Laura couldn't help that now. She peered around the tree and watched as a police cruiser pulled into the clearing in front of the cabin.

CPD, read the letters on the side. Chicago Police Department.

They'd turned north, crossed the border into Wisconsin last night, and here was a CPD car. What would a CPD car be doing in Wisconsin?

Laura bowed her head and offered up one frantic plea for help, for strength and for some semblance of calm.

Nick tried to call Drew as soon as he got into town and found a pay phone. The lines were busy. He drove around the tiny town and tried not to think about the fact that Laura and Rico were alone. He wished now that he'd brought them.

A few minutes later, he got through to Drew's office, but not to Drew himself. There was no way he was going to let some switchboard operator have his name to broadcast the fact that he'd called Drew, so he found the grocery store, stocked up on some supplies, then went back to the phone. At last Drew came on the line.

"It's me," Nick said, careful not to use his name.

"I was afraid you wouldn't check in today, and we've got some things to talk about. We ID'd the cop. William Welch Morris. He's the one who used to date Renata Leone, and I'm betting, from your description, he's the one who tried to take Rico out of the hospital."

"Tell me you caught him."

"No, but we have an APB out on him. We'll have him soon, but . . . there's something else, about yesterday. I should have told you last night, but things were so crazy. One of the policemen at the scene was hit. Nick, he died."

Nick swore. "I'm sorry, buddy."

Drew brushed off Nick's condolences and told him in a tightly controlled voice, "We'll have to deal with that a little later. For now, we're going to think about catching the man who did this to him. And, Nick?"

"Yes."

"Whoever did this is now wanted for killing a policeman. If these people weren't reckless before about trying to cover their tracks or shooting anything that moved, they will be now. They know what happens to people who take down an officer of the law."

"You're telling me they're ten times more dangerous than they were before?"

"Exactly. Now, tell me one more thing."

"Sure."

"You're calling from a pay phone?"

"Yes."

"Your... friends are in the car?"

"No."

"You came out alone and left your friends somewhere while you made the call?"

"Yes."

"Somewhere close by?"

"Don't start playing games with me now, Drew. What else aren't you telling me?"

"Where are they?" he asked, instead. "How far?"

"About fifteen minutes away." Nick knew now that he never should have left Rico and Laura. "What's wrong?"

"We had a possible sighting of Morris reported late yesterday, from a good source, a policeman in a little town in Wisconsin. He didn't see the APB or the sketch until after he'd already seen the man. Otherwise we would have Morris by now. He's not hard to spot. He's in a stolen CPD car. At least, we figure he was yesterday."

"Back up," Nick said, thinking about the miles between him and the cabin right now. "Wisconsin? Someone saw him in Wisconsin?"

"I'm afraid so. Tell me you're not in some little town in Wisconsin on the lake, a place called Wind Bay. Because if you're there, Morris must have followed you when you left Chicago yesterday."

Laura watched and listened while the cop searched the cabin, then came back outside. He had a cellular phone, and he was arguing with someone over the phone.

It wasn't hard to hear his end of the conversation. He knew he had the right place. Someone named Marty had trailed them when they left the apartment building yesterday. Marty was on the train with them. When they got off the train, this man now standing in the clearing of the cabin had been waiting in his police cruiser.

He'd followed them every step of the way.

Laura felt a nasty shiver work its way down her spine. Beside her, Rico started to whimper and rock back and forth like a baby trying to comfort himself.

She pulled him into her arms and scanned the dense woods ahead of them. She had no idea what lay beyond the trees. Lake Michigan was supposed to be off to the right, no farther than the length of a city block. The only road out was behind them, with a CPD car blocking the path.

She had no idea which way to run.

* * *

Nick drove like a madman to the edge of town and then east, toward the lake. When he first heard Drew's startling news, he simply put down the phone and nearly took off running toward the car.

Then, in a brief moment of sanity, he realized Drew didn't know where the cabin was. He gave him directions as best he could, then made himself stay on the line long enough to hear what he could expect from the FBI and the Chicago police.

The FBI had agents in the town already checking out the sighting reported late yesterday. Drew and a handful of other agents were coming in a helicopter. He wasn't sure how long that would take. He would radio the local sheriff's department and the FBI agents on the scene with the location of the cabin, and he wanted Nick to go to the sheriff's office immediately.

That was when Nick hung up on him and raced for his car. Now, as he went screaming down the two-lane road, he had time to think.

He shouldn't have left them. The three of them were in this together, and he never should have left them. More than anything, Nick hated the fact that the last thing he'd said to Laura was that he couldn't be the kind of man she needed or the father Rico deserved.

Laura saw the cop kick the tires on the police cruiser, then stalk off toward the woods.

She clamped her arms around Rico, who was still whimpering.

"Shh," she whispered in his ear. "Not now, little man. You can't make a sound right now. Understand? We have to be as quiet as mice."

And with that, she hunkered down behind the big tree and tried not to breathe.

The cop was coming closer. She didn't dare poke her head around the tree trunk and check to see just how close he was.

They had waited too long. Her indecision may have just ruined their chance of escape. Because now it was too late to run.

Nick came roaring down the dirt road toward the cabin. On the seemingly endless drive, he'd thought about how he should handle this. He could park in the woods before he reached the cabin and walk in. But that would take time he didn't think he had. And he didn't have a weapon, either. The cop would have a gun for sure, probably a knife, as well, like the one he'd used on Renata Leone.

If by some miracle the cop wasn't there yet, he'd drive up to the cabin, get Rico and Laura into the car and take off again.

If the cop was there . . .

Nick felt sick inside, just like the day he'd heard the first reports of the shooting in the hallways at Carter Barnes's expensive private school. Just like the moment he'd heard Carter had been the boy who'd pulled the trigger. Just like the day Jason Williams died.

He thought about poor Rico and the way he looked after the three of them had escaped from the cop outside the hospital, thought about how Rico looked in Laura's arms with her hand smoothing down his tight, brown curls. He thought about something in Rico's sad, brown eyes that looked curiously like trust. He couldn't betray the trust this little boy had placed in him.

And he thought about Laura and all he'd told her he couldn't give her and Rico.

It was crazy, but he felt as if he'd lived a lifetime in the past five days. Surely they deserved more than five days together.

Nick swore as the car sped through the trees. He never should have left them.

Laura had her hand held tightly over Rico's mouth, and she whispered with her mouth pressed against his ear in an effort to calm him.

The cop was nearby. She could hear the rustle of the leaves and the crackle of twigs under his feet as he made a slow sweep of the woods. He was so close. She didn't know what to do, and she felt like such a coward. They should have run as soon as the cop showed up. They should have gone with Nick or—

Laura cut off the thought. It was too late to be thinking of what she should have done, time now for deciding what she was going to do to keep this man from finding them.

He was even closer now, somewhere to their right and behind them. Any minute now she expected him to pop up behind them.

Laura saw a rock on the ground beside them, let go of Rico long enough to pick it up and hurl it into the woods behind them and to the left.

The rock tore through the tree limbs and the underbrush. Once it settled, she strained for some sound indicating the cop's movement. Finally, he started walking again. She couldn't tell which way he was going at first, then realized he was still coming toward them.

Laura picked up another rock and held on to it. If it came down to it, she might have a chance to bash the cop's head hard enough to knock him out.

She blinked back tears as she told Rico she had to let him go for a minute. She made him promise to run as fast as he could if he got the chance, then pushed him to the ground at the base of the tree.

Laura stood, her back pressed against the trunk of the tree, and listened. The cop was still moving toward them. She swallowed hard. She thought she could hear him breathing now he was so near.

With the rock in both her hands, she raised her arms above her head, ready to strike. She was shaking so much she was afraid she might drop it. Rico was sobbing softly again; the cop was bound to hear that.

Fresh, hot tears stung her eyes, and she didn't dare lower her arms to wipe them away.

It wasn't over yet, she reminded herself. This crazy cop hadn't won yet.

He was right on the other side of the tree. The sound of his movement was too close for him to be anywhere else. This would be her only chance.

She had a death grip on the rock. She was ready to spin around and strike, when she heard something that drowned out the soft sounds of footsteps or a little boy weeping.

It was a car! She heard a car roaring toward the cabin.

From the other side of the tree, the cop called out menacingly, "Rico! I'm not done with you, boy. I'll take care of whoever showed up, and then I'm coming back for you. You can run if you want to, boy, but you won't get far enough away from me to do you any good."

Laura waited a tense ten seconds to see if the cop was lying, then heard footsteps retreating through the woods. She dropped the rock and hauled Rico into her arms, doing her best to reassure him with her words and her touch that they weren't going to be here for the cop to find when he came back.

When he saw the police cruiser with the CPD logo on it, Nick nearly lost all control. He had this urge to ram his car into it just for sheer satisfaction. But he resisted. They might need one of these vehicles to get away—if they got the chance to run, that is.

He didn't see the cop anywhere. He didn't see anyone outside. Nick turned to the cabin, dreading what he might find inside.

Rico and Laura might not be there, he told himself. Laura might have heard the car coming and gotten herself and Rico out of the cabin in time. Still, his hand was shaking badly when he reached for the doorknob. Her image came to him when he closed his eyes.

Five days, he thought. Were they supposed to cram a lifetime into five days?

He swallowed hard and turned the knob. The door slid open, and he saw nothing. No one.

"Laura," he called out.

No response.

He should go in and check the bedrooms, he decided, his eyes drawn to two more doors. Then he'd check the woods in back, then the lake.

They were still there somewhere. Surely they were still alive. After all, Nick couldn't imagine the cop hanging around once he finished the job.

Nick fought the urge to be sick.

He heard a movement to the left, just as he was about to enter the cabin. He saw Officer William Welch Morris walk around the side of the cabin with a revolver in his hand.

Laura made herself count to sixty while the cop walked away. She held Rico's trembling body close to hers and tried to explain to him that in a minute they had to run. He was too big for her to carry, and it would slow them down too much if she tried. He had to stand up and run. She would be beside him all the way.

She didn't know who had pulled up to the cabin, and she didn't think they could afford to stay around and find out.

But when she stopped counting and stood, she looked back at the cabin and saw the car, Nick's car.

And then she didn't know what to do.

"Dr. Garrett," the cop said, waving the gun at him and smiling like a madman.

"Morris," Nick said, taking great pleasure in making the man uneasy by knowing his name.

"I should have killed you when I had the chance at the hospital," Morris said with a snarl.

"That would have been smarter than killing a policeman outside my apartment yesterday morning."

Nick took great pleasure in seeing signs of nervousness in the man. "Do you know how they treat people who kill law-enforcement officers? Do you know how hard the FBI and the police will work to try to catch you now? You don't have a prayer."

The cop pointed the gun at the center of Nick's chest and slipped off the safety with a soft click.

"Maybe you didn't notice, Doctor. I'm the one with the gun. You are the one who doesn't have a prayer."

"You'll never get out of here," Nick said, praying that it was true. "The FBI are coming in a helicopter. The local sheriff's department should be here any moment. I'm surprised we haven't heard the sirens yet."

"Nice try. I almost believed you at the hospital when you told me that, but it won't work today," the cop said, the gun still held dead center on Nick's chest. "The only FBI agent who knows I'm here is on my side."

"Actually, he's behind bars right now." Nick was lying. He had no idea whether the man had been caught yet. He didn't wait around long enough to find out. "But one of the county deputies spotted you yesterday on your way into town. He recognized you right away when he saw the sketch the FBI released when they issued an APB on you. By now everyone knows you're here."

The cop might have bought part of that story. Nick couldn't be sure. "If I were you," he continued, "I'd get the hell out of here—right now."

The man laughed. "If I go, you and the kid and the teacher are going with me."

Nick's heart nearly stopped beating then. If Morris wanted Rico and Laura to go with him, then surely that meant they were still alive. He wanted to ask, but what was the point? He wouldn't believe anything the man said anyway. For now, he had to wait it out. And he had to stay calm and keep the man talking, to buy some time until help arrived.

"Are you sure you have time for all that?" Nick asked. "If you don't go now, you won't get away. And you'll never get out of here with the three of us."

"No one is coming after me."

Nick shrugged. "Hey, it's your neck. Not mine."

The cop took a step closer. The gun was maybe ten feet from Nick's chest. "Right now, you'd be smart to worry about your own neck, not mine. You and I are going to take a walk in the woods."

"Why?"

"Because that's where the kid is."

Nick didn't think he had much choice right now. He started walking.

Laura stood on the other side of the cabin, listening. The sound of Nick's voice was one of the sweetest she had ever heard.

She was so relieved at first that she couldn't think about what to do next. And before she had a chance to figure it out, the two of them were walking toward her.

There was no time. Laura pressed herself against the wall. She had another rock in her hand. Maybe, if the man was close enough when he came around the side of the cabin, she could bash him over the head with this one.

If not, he would probably spot her.

At least he wouldn't find Rico right away. And maybe Nick was telling the truth. Maybe the FBI and the deputies were coming this time.

If not, then . . .

Laura stiffened and pressed herself as close as she could to the wall. Nick appeared from around the side of the cabin, maybe ten feet away from her. His steps faltered when he spotted her out of the corner of his eye, but he didn't turn toward her.

He looked furious, probably at her, but what was she supposed to do? Let this man shoot him?

Seconds later the cop was visible, as well. He had a huge gun in his hands, and it was pointed at Nick's back. Laura's rock looked puny in comparison. And the man was too far away for her to reach him.

Laura tried to not even breathe, sure the sound would give her away. The two men continued to walk toward the woods, where she had hidden Rico.

It would take them some time to find the boy, unless they got lucky, but the man had a gun.

She couldn't wait. She had to do something. And then . . . she heard the faint wail of the sirens.

The cop heard it, too. He turned around. Then this nasty gleam came into his eyes when he spotted Laura.

"Well, it's the teacher. And she has another rock." He held up his weapon. "I have a gun, and I want you to drop that."

Laura did.

"Come over here by the doctor. Nice and slow."

She walked to Nick's side. He took her hand in hers and squeezed it tight. There were a million things she wanted to say to him right now, but couldn't. She had to believe that they would have plenty of time to talk to each other later, after this man was caught.

"Now," the cop said, "where's the boy?"

"He ran to the lake," Laura said with as much conviction as she could muster. "I told him to go there when I heard Nick's car coming."

"The lake?"

Laura nodded. "I thought he might find someone there who could call for help."

"Lady, you're a lousy liar. And I don't have time for this. Where's the kid?"

"You don't have time to find him," Nick said. "I told you, the FBI are coming in a chopper. They know you stole the police cruiser yesterday, so it's going to be easy to find you on the road. If you're smart, you'll get out of here now."

The gun didn't waver, but the sweat was building on the man's brow with every wail of the sirens.

"Time is running out," Nick said.

"Shut up! Where's the boy?"

"I told you," Laura said, "he's at the lake."

"I don't think so," the cop said, then turned back toward the woods. "I heard him back there. I bet you were there with him. And I bet I can get him to come out."

Laura shut her eyes and listened to the sirens, which were coming ever closer. All they needed was another minute or two.

"Rico!" the cop yelled into the woods. "I've got your teacher here with me. You know what I'm going to do to her? The same thing I did to your mother if you don't get your butt out here right now!"

He pulled a knife from his left boot. "See?" He let the sunlight glint off the blade. "See what I have? Remember what this does, Rico?"

Laura prayed that the boy would stay where she'd left him, but she honestly didn't think he would.

"Where is he?" Nick whispered into her ear as the cop walked toward the woods.

"Buried under a pile of leaves. But if that man goes back there, he'll find him."

"Then we'll have to make sure he doesn't go back there."

"Nick?" Again there were so many things she wanted to tell him and no time to do it. She settled for an urgent request. "Be careful."

He stared back at her, the look in his eyes telling her that he had a lot of things he'd like to say, as well.

"We should have had more time," she said.

"We'll get it." He almost made her believe it. "Laura, if Rico comes out into the open, you hit the ground, all right?"

She nodded.

"Promise me."

"I will."

"Rico!" the cop shouted again, walking back toward Nick and Laura. "This is it! I'm through waiting. Come over here, teacher."

She swallowed hard and started to move. Nick wouldn't let go of her hand.

"No," he said.

The cop brought the gun around and pointed it toward Nick. He was getting more and more nervous as the sirens grew louder. "You know," the cop said, "you're right. I don't have time for this. And I'm going to kill you all anyway, so I might as well start right here with you."

Laura couldn't even scream. She opened her mouth, but nothing came out. Nick squeezed her hand. He was going to do something, but what could he do? What could she do? She didn't know. She—

"Wait!" From somewhere in the woods came the rustling of leaves and a little boy's cry.

Laura felt something shove her until she was off balance. She fell hard to the ground. Out of the corner of her eye, she saw Rico running out of the woods and saw Nick lunge at the gunman.

She screamed. Nick collided with the cop, but the cop still held on to the gun. Laura remembered Rico's trick from the hospital. She grabbed a handful of dirt and threw it into the cop's eyes.

The man choked and spit. He howled in outrage. In a reflex action his hand went to his eyes, and dropped the gun. Nick grabbed it and backed away toward Laura.

Nick was dirty from rolling on the ground. There was a trickle of blood coming from the side of his mouth. He had never looked better to her.

The cop was still howling and cursing. And Rico was standing frozen by the tree and crying.

Laura hesitated.

"Go on," Nick said. "He needs you right now."

The deputies were there in less than a minute. The whirling sound of a helicopter came soon after that. Nick handed over the gun, then went to the edge of the woods where Laura stood holding Rico.

Nick's heart was still racing painfully, his mind on those awful minutes before he arrived, when he didn't know if he would get there in time.

All of a sudden, he had no energy left. He'd been running on sheer nerves alone, and now even those deserted him.

Rico was crying. "He hurt my mother," he said.

"I know, little man," Laura replied.

"He killed her."

"Oh, Rico."

"Didn't he?"

Laura looked to him for guidance. Nick nodded.

"Yes," she told the boy. "I'm sorry. He did."

"I saw him after he did it. He said . . . he was going to get me, too. He chased me down the alley, and I just ran and ran and ran."

"It's all over now," Laura said with tears streaming down her face. "He won't be able to hurt you now."

"Really?"

"I promise. He's going to jail. He won't be able to get to you from there."

Rico turned back toward the cabin, to the woods, then back to Laura. His sad little face crumpled again as he started to weep. "But what . . . what's gonna happen to me?"

"I thought you might want to come home with me. And be my little boy. Or, my little man?"

Rico nodded vigorously. Laura hauled him back into her arms. "It's going to be all right," she told him. "I'll take care of you. I promise."

Laura looked over the top of the boy's head to Nick. She was crying even harder now. He reached out and wiped her tears away.

Then she held out an arm to him in invitation to join the two of them. Nick took one step, then another. He made it to her side. Her arm came around him, drawing him into the circle of the two of them, which now became a circle of three.

Chapter 14

Nick let three long weeks go by without touching her, without kissing her, without having her in his bed. He saw her only when Rico came twice a week for therapy sessions at the shelter, where Nick was volunteering again.

And he couldn't say why he stayed away or what he was waiting for to make him understand what he should do next.

He felt restless and uncertain—two entirely common emotions of late. But there was a difference now. The restlessness and the uncertainty bothered him. They gnawed at him. He wanted to do something, but what?

More than anything, he wanted to go to her. But what would he say?

Would she see him differently now that they weren't running for their lives?

They'd had only five days together. Five incredible, intense, life-altering days. At least, for him they had been.

He was a psychiatrist. He knew what fear and danger and adrenaline could do to people. All their emotions were heightened. Was that all it had been between them? Not for him.

At first, he thought he would give her some time, give this whole mess time to settle out.

Morris, along with another police officer and an FBI agent, were in jail awaiting trial. Among other things, Morris was charged with the murders of Renata Leone and a police officer.

Drew explained to them that Morris and his partner had indeed gotten a case of sticky fingers, helping themselves from time to time to seized drug money, sometimes to stolen property they recovered but never turned over as evidence. They'd helped themselves to drugs from time to time, as well.

Morris had met Renata Leone when he busted her supplier one night while Renata was there. He suspected she saw him take some of the heroin, and he found her the next day. They made a deal. He offered her some of his take if she would keep quiet. Occasionally, she led him to a dealer she thought might have a lot of cash on hand.

The partnership turned sour when Renata wanted out. She was under pressure from the social workers to get off the drugs for good or lose Rico. And she wanted to get away from Morris, but he wouldn't let her go.

One day, after she threatened to turn him in to the cops if he didn't leave her alone, Morris killed her. Rico found him as he was trying to get rid of the body.

And then Morris had to make a choice. Did he take the time to hide the body as best he could or go after the boy?

He chased Rico for blocks, but Rico got away. Not knowing where to turn, threatened with his life if he talked, Rico ran for three days before stumbling into the Hope House shelter.

By the time Morris returned to the alley, there were too many people around. He couldn't risk moving Renata's body. Luckily for him, it was days later before anyone found her.

He had time to search the apartment, and if Renata kept any written account of what happened between her and Morris, they would never know it. There was nothing left when the police searched.

Morris was facing two counts of murder.

Nick was something of a celebrity again. He and Laura and Rico had more than their fifteen minutes of fame. Of course the papers dredged up the whole story of Carter Barnes's shooting spree from a year ago. Carter's mother, who'd won her election, was running off at the mouth again about Nick. But Carter's mother wasn't the only one. Nearly a year after his death, Jason Williams's family was after the truth about what had happened to their son, and they came to Nick, among others, for answers.

Amazingly, the Williamses didn't blame Nick, and they weren't letting Carter Barnes's parents get away with blaming Nick publicly, either. The story that came out was vastly different from the one the television stations and the newspapers had run the summer before.

At first, Nick went into hiding from the reporters. The shooting in front of his apartment led reporters to that scene, so he abandoned it for a few days. He ended up sleeping in A.J.'s old room at the shelter, which was still empty because A.J.'s replacement hadn't been hired yet. And then he found himself working again.

He reclaimed a part of his old life, and it felt good. He was also helping Rico deal with his mother's death, which meant that twice a week, he and Laura greeted each other like polite strangers in the halls of the shelter, then talked after his session with Rico as if they had nothing more in common than an interest in the boy.

He thought she was even more beautiful, more desirable than before, if possible. He wanted so badly to touch her, to take her in his arms. And he had dreams about her—vivid, endless, erotic dreams.

Nick tried to keep busy. It shouldn't have been that difficult with a shelter full of kids, all in desperate need of help. He tried not to think about the things he'd never asked her, the things they never had time to discuss. He wondered if she'd think he lost his mind if he simply called and asked her out.

They'd never had a date, and here he was believing he was in love with her, wondering if she might possibly feel the same and how they might build a life together.

Funny, he'd never been shy around women, never been one of those men to fumble around for the right thing to say. But the past year had changed him. Not as much as he feared, thanks to Laura. But he wasn't the man he used to be.

He was still debating what to do, what to say to her, when he picked up the phone two days later and found her on the other end of the line.

"What's wrong?" He sensed instantly that something wasn't right.

"Rico is gone." Her voice was low and strained. "I thought . . . I didn't know who else to call."

Nick was glad she'd turned to him. "Tell me what happened."

"I went in the bedroom to take a call from the social worker. I don't like to talk in front of him because it upsets him. He knows it's up to the social workers and the judge to decide whether he gets to stay with me. I was on the phone for maybe ten minutes. When I came downstairs, he was gone."

"Okay, hang on, Laura. We'll find him. How long ago did this happen?"

"Nearly an hour."

"Did you call the police?"

"Do you think I should? I mean, do I have to bring them into it? He's still so afraid of them. He just can't understand that most of them aren't like Morris. If a police officer tried to pick him up, I don't know what he'd do."

"I don't know," Nick said. "Where do you think he'd go?"

"To see you, maybe. He talks about you all the time. He wants to know . . . why the three of us aren't together anymore."

Nick turned his face away from the receiver and swore. "Laura, if I could begin to explain it to you or to him I would, but I—"

"I didn't ask you for anything," she shot back. "Not even an explanation. I just . . . I want you to watch for him, in case he comes to find you. And, uh, call me if he does, all right?"

"Of course I'll call you." He was angry then, when he had no right to be. He had created this situation by avoiding her, by pushing her away. Clearly, he'd hurt her by doing that. And he'd hurt Rico, as well. "Is that all you want from me now? A phone call if I happen to find him?"

She didn't say anything for a long time. Then finally she added, "I don't want anything from you that you don't want to give. I don't want guilt. I don't want some sense of obligation. I don't want you to say anything that you don't mean or don't feel."

"Okay, tell me what you do want."

"Right now, I just want my little boy back."

"All right." As he had in those tense moments in back of the cabin with Morris and his gun on them, Nick thought of a million things he wanted to say right then. And he didn't think this was the time for any of them. He settled for "I miss you. Both of you."

"Well, you have a strange way of showing it, Doctor."

"I'm sorry."

"So am I. I . . . I can't talk to you about this right now. I have to find Rico."

"You need to stay there at the apartment. He might come back. Or he might call."

"I don't know if I can do that."

She sounded so afraid.

"I'd come and stay with you, but if you really think he's coming here, I should be here to talk to him. He must have something pretty important on his mind to take off like that."

"He—" Laura choked on the words. "This isn't the time to get into this. But, in case he comes, you need to be prepared."

"For what?"

"He thought you and I, or that the three of us, were going to be a family."

There was an opening he couldn't afford to pass up. "Do you still want that?"

Dead silence greeted him, and it went on for so long that he thought she'd gotten mad at him and simply walked away. Then he heard her put down the phone, or maybe she put her hand over the mouthpiece. Whatever she did, he was certain he heard the hushed sound of a woman weeping, and he felt like an absolute jerk.

"Laura, please, don't. It's going to be all right. I swear to you. We'll find Rico, and then we'll sit down somewhere together and we'll work this thing out. You'll see. I just need to—"

He turned his head toward a commotion in the hallway, saw one little boy break through the crowd of teenagers. Then the boy stopped and stared at him defiantly.

"He's here," he told Laura.

"Rico?"

"Yes. Right here in front of me, mad as hell—at me, I'm betting. But otherwise he looks fine."

"I'm on my way," she said.

"Laura?" he said, too late. She hadn't told him whether she, too, wanted the three of them to be together.

Surely that's what she wanted. Women didn't cry over men they didn't care about, did they? There was enough doubt in his mind to drive him a little crazy between now and the time she arrived.

Carefully, Nick put down the phone. He didn't have any more time to be uncertain, no more time for self-doubt. He had to turn and face the boy standing in the hallway.

"Friend of yours, Dr. Nick?" the teenager working the door that night asked him.

"Yes."

"He didn't want to tell us anything but that."

"I'll take care of him," Nick said, motioning for Rico to follow him down the hallway.

He didn't turn around to see if Rico followed. He didn't want to give him the upper hand. Nick took him upstairs to the room where he now slept, the one where Rico and Laura had spent that first night at the shelter.

Nick sat on the side of the bed, rested his elbows on his knees, his hands clasped in front of him, as he tried his best to appear relaxed.

Rico was mad enough for the two of them. Nick was trying to be reasonable about the whole thing.

"You've got some explaining to do, young man."

Rico shot him a sullen look that said he didn't have to explain anything to Nick. He had a premonition of what the years ahead, particularly the teenage years, would hold for the people raising this boy.

Nick laid into him. It was time he got used to the fact that he would be answering to someone for his behavior. "Did you ever think that someone might be worried to death when you ran off like this?"

"Nobody ever did before," Rico shot back.

"Well, a couple of people do now."

"Like who?"

"Laura, for one."

"That's one," he conceded, daring Nick to name someone else.

"And me."

The bravado was running thin at that point. Rico looked more like a scared little boy than anything else. Nick sensed that they had reached the crux of the problem.

"Want to tell me what was so important that you had to scare Laura half to death to come talk to me about it tonight?"

Rico scuffed one shoe against the other and remained silent.

"It must have been awfully important," Nick prompted. "Because I know you care about her. You know she loves you."

Rico stared at the floor. "I meant to leave her a note."

"Not good enough."

He glared at Nick. Nick wondered whether he would be insulting the boy's dignity if he gave him a quick hug. It was a toss-up with eight-year-old boys, with the urge to grow up warring with the tenderhearted kids inside them. Nick decided not to risk it at the moment.

"You know," he told Rico, "she was crying when she called to tell me you'd disappeared."

"She cries over you, too."

Nick straightened and took a breath. "I know. I found that out tonight, as well."

"I thought..." And then the little boy was sobbing.

Nick pulled Rico to him and held on tight. Rico stood stiffly in his arms at first, then finally gave in and let Nick hug him.

"Tell me what you thought, buddy."

"I thought we were going to be together. You know, like a real family."

"Is that what you want?"

Rico nodded, his tears still falling.

"I needed some time to think about that. It scared me a bit. I never had a little boy before."

"I never had a dad," Rico said.

Rico made it sound so simple, and maybe it was. Rico had never seen his father. It wouldn't be hard for Nick to do better than that.

"I had a dad for a while," Nick said. "He went away when I was a little younger than you are."

"Do you still miss him?"

"I do. Or, I miss the kind of dad I wish he had been. I miss the kind of dad some of my friends had."

"I still miss my mom. But Miss Laura is going to be my new mom, if the judge says it's okay."

"I know. I think it's going to work out just fine."

"So, what about . . . you know?"

"Me?"

Rico nodded.

"Laura is on her way over, and I think you and I need to work some things out before she gets here."

It took Laura forever to get across town to Hope House. And the whole time, she kept thinking of Rico making this journey again by himself, miraculously without running into some kind of trouble along the way.

Then once she arrived she had the hardest time making herself go inside. There was no telling what Rico had said to Nick, no telling what kind of answers Nick had given him.

She still couldn't believe she admitted to Nick that Rico wanted the three of them to be a family. She found that the height of humiliation.

He had to know how she felt about him, and he must have his reasons for staying away from her and Rico. Maybe he would tell her what those were. And maybe they could overcome them. Maybe they couldn't.

Either way, she had to walk into that shelter and listen to him explain these things to her. She wasn't sure she was up to facing him.

Funny, for the past three weeks she had longed for some word from him, some signal, some explanation. None had been forthcoming.

Now, here she was, about to get what she wanted, and she wasn't sure she was ready.

Laura swiped a hand past her cheeks, relieved to find them dry. She fidgeted with the clasp at the back of her neck that held her hair in place and smoothed her hair back from her face again.

She wondered if he'd look at her and know she'd cried off and on during the trip over, then remembered that it didn't matter if he did. He'd heard her crying on the phone already.

Her cheeks burned. She straightened her shoulders and marched inside. The teenager at the desk directed her upstairs to what she thought must be the room where Rico had spent his first night here. That seemed like a lifetime ago, though it had barely been a month.

Her legs felt like lead as she climbed the back stairs and walked down the hall. The door was closed. She put out a shaky hand to open it.

"Hi."

Startled, she turned toward that deep, husky voice she'd come to know as well as her own. Nick stepped out of the darkness at the end of the hall, where a bulb had burned out. "Hi."

"Rico is fine. I tried to get him to go to sleep, but he was reluctant."

"Nightmares," Laura explained. "He still has nightmares."

Nick nodded. "He didn't run into any trouble on the way over here."

Laura felt marginally better. She took a breath, hoping to steady herself, but still had the shakes.

Nick looked ... uneasy. He looked a little tired, a little tense, but otherwise wonderful. He was such a striking man. She always forgot that, always found it a little unsettling to see him at first. His dark hair, his eyes, that determined set to his jaw—they all came together in a way that had her catching her breath and making rash promises to herself about not making a fool of herself over him.

Of course, it was probably too late for that now.

She thought about the brief hours they'd spent together during those two nights, the way she'd held back nothing when she was in his arms, the way their bodies fit together as if they were made for each other.

And then it was over. Like the best of dreams, the worst of nightmares, the whole thing had flown by. Sometimes she had trouble believing it ever happened. Then she closed her eyes and saw his face. Her heart felt as if someone held it in his hands and squeezed it, the pain a tangible thing.

"I'll give him a few minutes." She looked at her watch, because that was safer than looking at Nick. "Then I'll need to take him home."

Nick nodded. "That should give us enough time to talk."

Laura closed her eyes and hoped some mysterious source of strength would come to her right then. It didn't. She felt as shaky as she had outside the shelter.

"Come over here." Nick tilted his head toward the darkness at the end of the hallway, toward the big, double-paned window there.

Laura managed to force her legs to move. As she passed him, he turned to walk beside her. His hand settled lightly against the small of her back, and she couldn't help it. She fought not to react in any way, but he must have felt her tense.

Nick pulled his hand away. She watched him struggle to keep his expression blank.

"This is very difficult for me," she said.

"I know. Do you hate me now?"

It would be so much easier if she did. "No, I just don't understand. And I guess I'm not even entitled to an explanation from you—"

"Yes, you are."

"Well then, I'm not sure if I'm up to hearing it right now."

"I missed you."

He'd said it like a man in anguish. Laura felt a little better. "We missed you, too."

"I don't know what happened. Everything was so simple when we were running away from that madman, and then it wasn't anymore."

"Nick, does this have anything to do with the fact that Rico is biracial?"

"No."

"Sorry, I had to ask."

"He could have purple stripes and pink polka dots. It wouldn't matter to me."

"Then what's wrong?"

"There was so much I wanted to say to you, but at the same time, there was so much I hadn't figured out for myself yet. And I didn't want to come to you with nothing but doubts and questions and uncertainties. But, Laura, those are all on my part. They're inside me. They don't have anything to do with you or Rico."

"Is this about your father?"

"I guess it is."

"Whatever he did to you, however he hurt you, you're not going to be anything like him, Nick. Surely you know that."

"It's taken me a while to figure that out. And I'm sorry it took so long, sorry that you got hurt in the process while I was trying to get my head on straight."

"Just tell me next time, okay? You can have as much time as you need—just let me know what's going on."

"You're a very generous woman, Laura. I was afraid that generosity might have run out where I was concerned." He reached for her hand. "I did miss you."

"That's a good start."

"I never stopped wanting you. I never stopped needing you. I thought somehow you'd know that, but..."

She shook her head, amazed by what she was hearing. "You never said any of those things to me."

"You mean I never told you I love you? Laura?" He turned her face up to his with two fingers on her chin. "You never said it to me, either. Did you think I'd just know? Or is love not a part of this?"

"It is. At least, on my side it is. I didn't think I had to say it. I thought I'd given it away in a dozen ways, at a dozen different times."

Nick shook his head then, and she thought she saw the glint of tears in his beautiful, dark eyes.

"Tell me," he whispered, his lips coming to meet hers.

"I love you, Nick. I always will."

"I love you, too, sweetheart."

"What are you going to do about it?" she asked.

He kissed her once, hard, fast, deep. She had trouble letting go of him when he was done.

"I just got scared, Laura. That night at the cabin, thinking about what a mess I'd made of my life and then trying to take on the responsibilities of raising a kid who was starting out with as many problems as Rico had—I just got scared. And I kept thinking about my own father. He was such a mess, and he always told me I'd never amount to anything. I never believed it until last year after Jason Williams died.

"My father told me something else I started to believe, as well. He left me and my mother when I was younger than Rico, and I found him a couple of years ago because I wanted to talk to him. When I asked him why he left, he said he didn't know anything about being a father. His father was never around when he was growing up. He claimed I'd understand someday. I'd be a father, too, and he doubted I'd manage the job any better than he had. After all, look at the example he set for me."

"You can't believe that's true, Nick."

"For one awful night, when I wanted you so badly I couldn't think straight, when I considered what was at stake, I thought about letting you down, letting Rico down. I thought about what a mess I'd made of my life this past year, and I believed it."

"And what about now?"

Nick smiled at her then. "Rico said something that made it all seem so simple. I told him I didn't know a lot about being a father, and he said that was all right, because he didn't know much about having a father."

"He doesn't. His father took off when he was still in diapers. Rico doesn't have any memory of him."

"I can do a lot better than that," Nick said. "I'm here, and I'm not going anywhere. I'd never leave him the way his father left him or the way my father left me."

Laura didn't know what to say to that. She couldn't quite speak anyway.

"I'm working again," Nick said. "Here at the shelter, and I got a call today from a friend of mine whose psychiatric practice has grown too big for him to handle. He's looking for a partner. He wants that partner to be me."

"Nick, that's wonderful. You want to do that? You're ready?"

"I think I am. Jason Williams's parents came to see me, and we talked. They don't blame me for his death, and they helped me see a lot of things differently. Of course, they didn't do nearly as much for me as you and Rico did. Rico thinks the three of us should be a family," Nick said. "What do you think?"

"I . . . I can see some merit in that idea."

"Can you see a ring, my ring, on your finger?"

"I'd like to see that."

"What if you saw me get down on one knee and beg?"

"I'd listen to what you had to say."

"What if I told you Rico is playing video games in the basement and there's a room down the hall with a bed in it and a lock on the door?"

"I'm open to suggestions."

He took her hand and tugged until she followed him down the hallway. Inside the room, the lights were out. He pulled her through the open door, closed it, locked it, then held her against it as his mouth claimed hers.

He made her dizzy, made her weak, made her want him so badly she ached with it.

"I don't know how I got so lucky to have you and that little boy stumble into my life," he said. "I don't know what I would have done without you, sweetheart."

Laura felt the tears come into her eyes. "I was coming after you tomorrow."

"I don't know if I would have made it through another day. You probably would have found me camped out on your doorstep the next morning."

He kissed her again, a kiss to get lost in. When it was over, they were both struggling for breath. Nick was eyeing the bed in the corner with a grin that had her trembling in anticipation. His body was pressed against hers, and the feel of it left her with no doubt about what he wanted to do next.

"I forgot to tell you the reason we came in here," he said. "There's one more thing Rico wants. A little brother."

* * * * *

Be sure to look for SECOND FATHER, the next captivating novel from Sally Tyler Hayes, available in December from Silhouette Intimate Moments.

There's nothing quite like a family

The new miniseries by
Pat Warren

Three siblings are about to be reunited.
And each finds love along the way....

HANNAH
Her life is about to change now that she's met
the irresistible Joel Merrick in HOME FOR HANNAH
(Special Edition #1048, August 1996).

MICHAEL
He's been on his own all his life. Now he's
going to take a risk on love...and
take part in the reunion he's been
waiting for in MICHAEL'S HOUSE
(Intimate Moments #737, September 1996).

KATE
A job as a nanny leads her to Aaron Carver,
his adorable baby daughter and the
fulfillment of her dreams in KEEPING KATE
(Special Edition #1060, October 1996).

Meet these three siblings from

Silhouette SPECIAL EDITION®

and

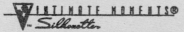
INTIMATE MOMENTS®

The Calhoun Saga continues...

in November
New York Times bestselling author

NORA ROBERTS

takes us back to the Towers and introduces us to
the newest addition to the Calhoun household,
sister-in-law Megan O'Riley in

MEGAN'S MATE
(Intimate Moments #745)

And in December
look in retail stores for the special collectors'
trade-size edition of

THE
Calhoun
Women

containing all four fabulous Calhoun series books:
COURTING CATHERINE,
A MAN FOR AMANDA, FOR THE LOVE OF LILAH
and *SUZANNA'S SURRENDER.*
Available wherever books are sold.

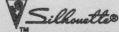

A woman with a shocking secret.
A man without a past.
Together, their love could be nothing less than

Scandalous

The latest romantic adventure from

CANDACE CAMP

When a stranger suffering a loss of memory lands on
Priscilla Hamilton's doorstep, her carefully guarded secret
is threatened. Always a model of propriety, she knows that
no one would believe the deep, dark desire that burns
inside her at this stranger's touch.

As scandal and intrigue slowly close in on the lovers, will
their attraction be strong enough to survive?

Find out this September at your favorite retail outlet.

What do you get when you take a
reluctant dad and match him up
with a determined mom?

A Baby?
Maybe

Discover how three couples are brought together
because of a baby and find that a little love goes
a long way.

Three complete stories of instant families by some
of your favorite authors:

RELUCTANT FATHER
by Diana Palmer

BORROWED BABY
by Marie Ferrarella

PASSION'S CHILD
by Ann Major

Available this October wherever
Silhouette and Harlequin books are sold.

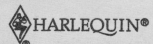 

Your very favorite Silhouette miniseries characters now have a BRAND-NEW story in

Brought to you by:

LINDA HOWARD

DEBBIE MACOMBER

LINDA TURNER

LINDA HOWARD celebrates the holidays with a **Mackenzie** wedding—once Maris regains her memory, that is....

DEBBIE MACOMBER brings **Those Manning Men** and **The Manning Sisters** home for a mistletoe marriage as a single dad finally says "I do."

LINDA TURNER brings **The Wild West** alive as Priscilla Rawlings ties the knot at the Double R Ranch.

Three BRAND-NEW holiday love stories...by romance fiction's most beloved authors.

Available in November at your favorite retail outlet.

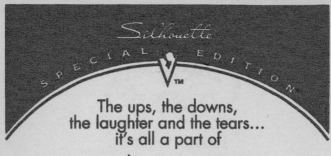

Silhouette

SPECIAL EDITION ™

The ups, the downs, the laughter and the tears... it's all a part of

PARENTHOOD
Diana Whitney

Stories that will touch your heart and make you believe in the power of romance and family. They'll give you hope that true love really *does* conquer all.

DADDY OF THE HOUSE (SE #1052, September 1996) tells the tale of an estranged husband and wife, who can't seem to let go of the deep love they once shared...or the three beautiful—and mischievous—children they created together.

BAREFOOT BRIDE (SE #1073, December 1996) explores the story of an amnesiac bride who is discovered by a single dad and his two daughters. See how this runaway rich girl becomes their nanny and then their mother....

A HERO'S CHILD (coming March 1997) reveals a husband who's presumed dead and comes home to claim his wife—and the daughter he never knew he had.

You won't want to miss a single one of these delightful, heartwarming stories. So pick up your copies soon—only from Silhouette Special Edition.